Snow

KRISSY V

This book is dedicated to all those budding ballerinas out there!

There are many ways to dance and not all of them conventional.

Just keep smiling and keep dancing if it's what you love to do.

En Pointe – On the tips of the toes

Pas De Chat – Is a classical ballet term meaning 'cat step." It gets it's name because the step resembles how a cat jumps.

Pique Turns - A dancer doing a **piqué** tour, or **piqué turn**, will step directly on to a full point (when in pointe shoes) or a high demi-pointe right as they begin the **turn** onto that same leg. A **piqué turn** can be done with the working leg in passé (both front and back), in arabesque, attitude or any other position that may be given.

Prologue

The lights go off … The audience is silent … The music starts off softly and I move en pointe in small, fluid movements out onto the stage. That's 'on the tips of my toes' for those of you who haven't danced ballet. This is my favourite part of the whole performance; the feeling of entering a stage with a captive audience who are waiting for me to shine.

It's still in darkness, and as I move to the middle of the stage, moving my arms up and down like the swan that I am, I get excited knowing that the light is going to shine on me and I'm going to continue en pointe and turn around to face the audience.

My feet will hurt like a bitch; they always do

after this part of the dance, but I have to dance through the pain. I can bathe them later when I'm resting. Ethan will massage them for me; he is fantastic at massaging my feet while I massage his.

It is such an emotional dance; I have to make sure my emotions show on my face as well as in my dancing. 'The Dying Swan' is my pièce de résistance. I love dancing in *Swan Lake* and have been the main swan for the last three years. I dance with the New York Ballet, and that's where I met Ethan.

Ethan is the love of my life. He is a ballet dancer as well, and he is so sexy, kind, and considerate. We travel around the world, dancing in ballets and living our lives in some of the most prestigious hotels and cities around the globe.

I met Ethan when I had just arrived in New York and we hit it off immediately. I am now living the dream!

Nothing could ever be better than this moment. The dance is coming to an end. I'm down on the stage, waving my arms about as the swan dies. The lights go out and the audience goes wild. I can see a standing ovation. This is for me! This is the best feeling in the world ... This moment, right now!

As the curtain goes down, I stand and walk off the stage. Seeing Ethan in the wings, I collapse into his arms. The dance is soul consuming and has taken every last bit of emotion out of me.

"You were amazing, babe. I love you." He holds me tight and whispers into my ear.

"Thank … thank you." I'm out of breath. "I love you too. Now go and knock them dead." He kisses me quickly and then starts to move towards the stage. I watch for as long as I can before I have to leave the wings.

After we have bowed and curtsied on the final curtain, we go to our dressing room and sit on the couch. It always takes us about half an hour to come down from the adrenaline buzz before we can get changed and leave the theatre. There is a bottle of champagne waiting for us, and Ethan opens it with a flourish.

Sitting and sipping our champagne, Ethan says, "I love life right now, Snow. We have an amazing life. I love you more than anyone I've ever known. Will you marry me?"

Wow, did he just propose to me?

"Oh my God, Ethan! Yes!" I almost scream in his face. He places a ring on my finger. I didn't even know he was holding it up to me. I kiss him and then start jumping all over the place.

The dressing room door opens and Melly runs in. "What's going on?"

"Ethan proposed. I said yes."

She starts screaming too. "Snow. Snow!" She's not jumping up and down like I thought she would. She looks worried.

"I know! It's so fantastic! I can't wait to ring my mum and tell her. She'll be so excited!" I say, moving towards her for a hug.

"No, Snow …" she says, pointing to the robe I'm wearing.

Looking down, I see there's blood running down my legs. "What's happening to me?"

I start screaming and then I pass out.

NUTCRACKER

"Come on, Snow! Point those toes! Where's your arch?" Ms. Selena shouts at me. She always shouts at me. "Snow! En pointe, NOW!"

I swallow down the tears that form every time I'm in this class. Ms. Selena is a horrific person. She makes the best dancers feel like they are awful. She's harder on me because I'm so tall. Too tall, she says. I don't think she likes me.

"Snow, you'll never be picked for the main roles because there will never be a man taller than you. This is going to be a stopping point in your career. You'd be better off doing a different style of dance. Ballet isn't for you." This falls from her lips regularly.

However, when she says this, it always makes me more determined to be the best ballet dancer in the world. I intend to travel the world dancing; it's all I know and all I need in my life.

Ms. Selena breaks through my thoughts. "Snow, show me your arch! If you can't then you won't be in the end of year recital. NOW!"

I arch my foot to within an inch of my life. It hurts so much, but I smile and give her what she wants.

Her lips lift at the edges into a semi-smile; that's the most I've ever had. I try not to smile back at her, and as quick as it came across her face, it's gone again. She doesn't show any emotion. We're taught from a very early age to only show emotion during our recitals.

We're in our final year at Sadler's Wells and there is a large production in the pipeline. *The Nutcracker* is one of my favourite dances, and I'm going to be auditioning for the main part - Clara.

"You'll never get those sought after roles, Snow, if you don't arch your foot properly." She shakes her head, and I point my toes even more. I can feel the pain in my tendons on the sole of my foot as they start to tighten. I know the pain is going to be horrendous, but I keep pointing, knowing that, without the pain, I'm not doing it right.

"Keep working on it," she says, as she moves over to Melly to see her arch. "Fantastic, Melly. Your arch is fabulous, as always."

Sneaking a peak over at Melly, I see her arch is nowhere near as good as mine. It makes me so mad that Ms. Selena doesn't like me and goes out of her way to hate me and what I'm able to achieve.

I'm not your average ballet dancer. Petite, pale, hair pulled in a tight bun, pink ballet pumps; a puppet on Ms. Selena's strings. That describes Melly, but it doesn't describe me.

Being six foot tall, stocky build, and dark-skinned with extremely untamed hair makes me stand out. I have an afro at the moment, but I add in different colours according to my mood. A lot of people describe me as Amazonian – I like it; it makes me sound tough and strong. So unlike a ballerina. That's why Ms. Selena doesn't like me.

After class, we change then Melly and I walk to the coffee shop on the way home. She links her arm through mine. "Come on, Snow.

Don't worry about Ms. Selena. She's just a bitch."

"She likes you, though, and we all know my arch was better than yours." I nudge her so she knows I'm joking.

"You have the best arch in the class. We all know that."

Walking into the coffee shop, we order our drinks and sit down to wait for them. Dancers aren't really allowed coffee so we always order decaffeinated; it feels like a good compromise.

"When did you say the auditions are for *The Nutcracker*?" I ask, dying to know.

"They're on Tuesday next week. Ms. Selena is giving us all the day off to go to the auditions. I think that cow Portia will be there too. She gets everything, you know, so we probably won't be lucky this time either."

"Fuck! She is such a bitch. Do you remember the last auditions? She pushed Suzie and made her fall over during her pirouette."

"Oh, God. Yeah, I forgot that. Bitch!"

We spend half an hour talking about all the horrible things Portia has done. She doesn't go to Sadler's Wells, she attends the London Russian Ballet School. They are extremely strict and their dancers are fantastic - you could never take that away from them - but God, they are princesses.

Melly and I met at our very first ballet class. No one would talk to me because I was so different to everyone else. Portia was there and she kept trying to trip me up and make me look stupid. Melly stuck up for me and we've been best friends ever since.

ONE WEEK LATER

Approaching the Royal Opera House, where the Royal Ballet always dance, its beauty never ceases to amaze me. It looks slightly Grecian from the outside, with its huge pillars and ornate ceilings that are beautifully lit up. Entering through a side door which says 'backstage' above it, we're guided to a registration table where we give our names and are subsequently given a number. Following the guide out to the auditorium, we see a lot of people are already here.

My breath catches just looking at the rows and rows of red velvet seats, gold balconies, and numerous chandeliers. You can see why it's an amazing place to perform. Sitting next to Melly, we watch in awe of some of the more experienced dancers. "We don't stand a chance," she whispers in my ear.

"Never say never, Melly," I whisper back, and take hold of her hand.

It is amazing to watch our friends dance on this beautiful stage, and we don't realise we've been sitting with our mouths open for the last hour. We only close them when my number is called. Melly gives me a kiss and I walk nervously towards the stage and up the stairs at the side.

One of the four judges says, "Tell us who you are, where you dance, and something interesting about you."

This is it … this is the one time I have to be smart and get them to remember me.

"My name is Snow." I take a deep breath; I'm really nervous. This is so important to me. This is my moment to make something of all the years I've spent concentrating on my dancing. "I dance at Sadler's Wells, and today…" I take another breath. "I am going to blow your minds."

I hear the judges gasp and I see Melly put her hand over her mouth. I don't know if she's trying to stop herself from laughing or if she thinks I've just made the biggest mistake in my short career. I don't care … I'm going to dance my socks off, and if I don't get the job then it's not for the lack of trying.

"Okay then. Show us what you've got!" one of the judges says, with a smile on his face.

Nodding, I curtsy and then stand in the middle of the stage. I love the Dance of the Sugarplum Fairy, and I know this dance inside and out as I've been dancing it at home since I was able to walk. My mum was a ballerina, and I used to love watching her perform, begging her to teach me. She stopped performing when she had me, though.

The lights go off … the music starts. With each beat, I raise my arms higher and flick my hands out, like a swan flapping its wings. Then I point my feet to each beat. When the music ramps up in speed, I do a pas de chat and flick my feet up to my knees. It's so dainty and fluid. It's like a jump in which each foot in turn is raised to the opposite knee.

I continue the dance to perfection. When I do my pique turns in a full circle around the stage, I can hear a few people take a deep breath. This is one move I *know* I'm good at. You could say they're my speciality. I don't get dizzy and I don't lose the momentum.

When I stop, the dance is over and some of the audience start clapping, knowing a good pique turn when they see one.

I bow and curtsy and then leave the stage. As the lights come up, I can see the judges talking amongst themselves. They're nodding and the male judge is smiling. Fingers crossed that's a good sign.

As I walk back to my seat, Melly stands up and hugs me. "That was fucking awesome! So much better than Portia! How the fuck am I going to dance and make an impression now, bitch!"

She laughs so I know she's only joking. Her number is called and she goes up on stage.

"Tell us who you are, where you dance, and something interesting about you," the same judge says.

She looks at me. "My name is Melly, I dance at Sadler's Wells, and I have to follow that!" she says, pointing at me.

"Okay. Take your position."

Melly does a fabulous job; she is very classical and her lines are perfect.

When she comes back down, I stand and hug her, like she did to me.

"Well done, Melly. You were amazing. I hope we both get places. I'm sure Portia will get the lead role like she always does, but there must be something for us in the ensemble."

"Let's wait and see. They'll tell us after the

last audition. Let's go get a drink."

Leaving the auditorium, we get a bottle of water from the concession stand in the foyer. I love this theatre; it's so full of character, and in the hallway there are lots of photographs of dancers and performers. We spend a lot of time looking at them before making our way outside.

There are quite a few girls already outside with drinks, leaning up against the wall. We've seen most of the girls before. Some are from Sadler's Wells, some are from the Russian Ballet School, and some are from the Royal Ballet School.

We hang around outside for a couple of hours. These things always take so much time. Then, a stocky gentleman comes outside and says, "Right, ladies. It's time to find out your fate!"

Everyone goes from being really quiet to chatting and whispering. After piling back into the theatre, the judges have moved from being in front of the stage to being on stage. They don't look as intimidating now, but they all look stern and none of them break a smile. It obviously takes a certain type of person to be a judge in the dance world.

"Thank you, ladies and gentlemen, for

coming down here today to audition," says a tall lady who has her hair tightly scraped off her face in a bun. I can tell she was, or even still is, a ballerina, as she has the correct poise and deportment.

After she sits down, the man sitting next to her stands up. At a guess, I would put money on him being a choreographer or director.

"So, let's get to the point of today. We're going to be taking *The Nutcracker* on tour, starting off in London in five months' time." He pauses, waiting for the excitement to die down. He doesn't speak until everyone is silent. "We want to use this as an opportunity to showcase the 'new era of dancers', the up and coming ballerinas. We will visit five countries and we will end up in New York a year later. If this interests you then please stay, but if this is a commitment you are not able to fulfil, please leave now." He sits down.

The once silent auditorium awakens once again with voices. There is a lot of shuffling, and we turn around to see what's going on. Some of the dancers are standing and shaking their heads, then they grab their coats and walk out of the auditorium. I gasp. These people are walking away from such a great opportunity.

"Melly, can you believe these people are leaving? I wonder why."

She stands up and grabs one girl's arm. "Hey, why are you leaving?"

The girl looks at her and says, "No way are my parents going to let me out of the UK without them. It sucks, but there's no point going any further." She picks up her bag and walks away, leaving the auditorium.

"Wow, Snow. This is what we've been working so hard for – why give that up so easily?"

"I know. I just hope, if it comes to it, my parents will let me go!" I cross my fingers and Melly does the same.

It takes about fifteen minutes for the auditorium to quieten down. Those who are out have left which means the dancers who are still here are the ones who are serious about this opportunity.

The man on the stage smiles as he looks around at the much-reduced group staring back at him.

"That narrows the goalposts a bit. So, obviously, we haven't cast everyone into specific roles yet, but there were a few that stood out to us."

He spends the next half an hour calling out

the list of names of people they want to be involved in the show. Melly's name is called out. So is Portia's, but I'm still sitting here, waiting. Maybe I blew it by being cocky. I could kick myself.

Melly grabs my arm, startling me. "Oh my God, Snow! Oh. My. God!"

"What? What did I miss?"

"They just called your name, stupid!"

"How the fuck did I miss that? I was daydreaming!"

"Hang on, he's still talking!" she says, finally letting go of my arm.

"That concludes the list. For those of you who didn't make it this time, it doesn't mean you won't make it next time. Keep dancing, keep auditioning, and you will achieve your dreams. For those of you who did make it, can you all stay so we can discuss more details with you?"

The whole auditorium erupts with people congratulating others. Some are crying and some are hysterical. After the ones who didn't make it have moved out, there's still a large group of us left. We all move so we're sitting in the front few rows.

A third judge stands. She is stern-looking, and I recognise her from one of my interviews at The Royal Ballet.

"Good afternoon, dancers," she says, with a sharp tone in her voice. She doesn't look happy that she has to talk to us, but she needs us. "We will be taking the rest of today to try and place each of you as a character. Some of you stood out and we have to decide which parts you would be able to portray. Others will be cast in the ensemble. Just remember, each role is as important as the next. We would like to reconvene tomorrow morning at nine-thirty in our studio at the back of the theatre." She sits back down and starts to gather her belongings.

The man stands up again. "Congratulations to you all. This is going to be hard work, and some of you will give up, but believe me, this will all be worth it in the end. When you go home today, think about the characters and see which one you would like to dance the most. Girls, you can't all pick Clara." He laughs. "We have that position filled already!" He sits back down and starts to get his belongings together too.

Looking at Melly, I can see Portia standing behind her with the biggest smile on her face. She's probably going to be cast as Clara and she knows it.

"See you tomorrow. I can't wait to start

rehearsing," she says, putting her things back into her bag. Her friends start hugging and congratulating her. "I'm so surprised you were picked, Snow, but then again, they need someone to be the Mouse Queen."

She is such a bitch!

"Come on, Snow. We have a lot of thinking to do!" Melly hugs me.

We turn to pick up our bags when Portia reaches out and grabs my arm.

When I look at her, she says, "I suppose they wanted the token black dancer for extra marketing or something, otherwise I'm sure you wouldn't be on the list." She flips her hair and walks off. Thank God, because I was ready to punch her.

Melly touches my arm. "Snow. Don't worry about her. She's so worried that, after your performance today, she won't get a lead part, but you will. She wouldn't live it down!"

I smile at her. I know she's only trying to make me feel better, but Portia might be right.

"Listen, Snow, we got places, and I really don't care who I am as long as I'm on that stage. I wonder where we'll travel to."

"I don't care. Anywhere would be amazing, but we're going to end up in New York, Melly. That is freaking unbelievable."

When we get home, we spend the rest of the evening dancing around the house and speculating which characters we can be. We talk to our parents about allowing us to travel around the world. They are behind us every step of the way. They know this is what we've been working up to for the last ten years or more.

When I go to bed, it's with a huge smile on my face.

I know that tomorrow, my life will change forever.

WORLD TOUR

After one week of gruelling rehearsals, we were all brought together and told which characters we were portraying. The biggest surprise of all was that I got the position of Clara. I couldn't believe it! This was the best thing that had ever happened to me. Portia was so mad, she stormed out of the theatre. She soon came back when she realised they weren't going to change their minds. She kept glaring at me, though. It was very unnerving.

After the first week of rehearsals and training, they paired me up with Christian. They had tried a couple of the other guys, but they didn't suit my style of dance, or they were too short. Ms. Selena's words came back to haunt me. I thought they were getting frustrated, but they brought Christian in especially. Firstly, because he's an amazing dancer, but secondly, because he is taller than me. Only by an inch, but it's a very important inch.

Christian is blonde-haired, six foot one, his muscles are really well-defined, and when he holds me, I just want to swoon. The best thing is that we're so well-matched dance-wise; we work well as a team. We become best friends, and along with Melly, we spend a lot of time together.

Eventually, we start performing for real audiences, not just our parents and school friends. The feedback is unbelievable.

"Praise to the new prima donna, Snow. She moves with such grace and beauty."

"The chemistry between Christian and Snow adds to this beautiful story."

"Is this pairing the new Fonteyn and Nureyev?"

The press speculate on our personal

relationship. They believe that because we dance so well together and spend all our spare time together, that we're dating.

Christian is absolutely gorgeous and I have really grown to love him over the last ten months of working with him, but he's not interested in me in that way. He prefers Max, the five foot eleven, dark-haired dancer who is playing the king.

The four of us, including Melly, hang around together after the shows and it gives everyone the impression that we're a happy foursome. Christian believes that it will bring bad press to the ballet if he tells everyone he's gay.

Travelling for the last nine months has been gruelling, but we've visited Paris, Berlin, Amsterdam, Copenhagen, Oslo, Stockholm, and we are about to do a two week stint in Moscow. Going to Russia, the home of ballet, is like Charlie turning up at Willy Wonka's Chocolate Factory ... dream come true territory!

As the plane comes in to land, it's quite bumpy, and I grab hold of Melly's hand. She laughs. "Are you still afraid of flying after all the flights we've had over the last few months?"

"Don't laugh, Melly. Yes, I am. The doctor gave me some tablets to calm me down, but I don't have any left. I could get into trouble if they know I take them, but it's only when I fly."

She laughs. "Why don't you see a doctor when we get to the hotel in Moscow, then you'll have them for when we fly to New York. I can't believe that we've been away from home for nine months, and I can't believe that we're going to be touching down in New York in two weeks' time."

"I know. I might do that. I really miss Mum, but I'm so excited about New York. Mind you, we have Moscow to enjoy first!"

"We sure do, and it's going to be a great experience."

"Please remain in your seats until the plane has come to a standstill," the air hostess says.

Of course, everyone starts to stand up as soon as the plane has stopped and then the aisle gets packed with people. We wait until everyone has left the plane before we stand, grab our bags, and follow the crowds.

Collecting our bags from the carousel, we meet everyone outside as we get on a bus that is waiting for us. Once we're sitting in our seats, Christian leans over and says, "You know I love you, right?"

I smile at him and reach over and touch his hand. "Yeah, baby." I call him baby now and again so people think we're a couple.

"I've decided that when we get to New York, I want to tell everyone that I love Max and we're in a relationship. I'm sick of hiding it. I love him and want to be able to tell everyone, and to be with him in public."

"Oh my God, that's fantastic. I'm so happy for you, Christian. You deserve this happiness." I pull him down so I can kiss him. I really do love him and want him in my life forever. I'd miss him if he wasn't.

"Thanks, babe. I just don't want you to get any bad publicity. You know, when people find out I'm gay and you knew about it. People assume we're in a relationship. They might think I lied to you."

"Don't worry about me, Christian. We haven't duped anyone. We love each other and that comes across in our dancing. When we were paired up, they certainly knew what they were doing." I lean over and kiss him on the cheek again.

We get close to the Ritz-Carlton Hotel, and I can feel the buzz of excitement building. Although we have to go to the theatre tonight, to walk the stage and get a feel of it, we will also be going out and looking around. We never drink when we're performing; we save it for the end of the tour and then we go mad and party.

Moscow doesn't disappoint us. We get rave reviews and plenty of offers to come back. We party hard at the end of the show; drinking, dancing, and singing. The vodka is fantastic and we get very well acquainted with it and the bottom of the toilet. We can't wait to come back another day.

NEW YORK, NEW YORK

After landing at JFK, I'm absolutely wrecked. It was a ten and a half hour flight. I can't wait to get to the hotel so I can go to bed.

Rehearsals start with a vengeance tomorrow as we have our first performance in two days.

"Christian, I'm so excited about dancing at the Lincoln Center. It's where the New York Ballet Company dances. You never know where this might lead us."

"I know, babe. I think I might wet myself."

"Fuck off, you dry shite!" I say, punching him in the side.

"Seriously though," he says, laughing and

holding his side. "I know this is so important to the next stage in our careers. I wonder if there will be any scouts watching."

"I know, it's so exciting. I would love to dance for the New York Ballet. It would be like a dream come true," I say, closing my eyes and dreaming a little.

"This could be the end of an era though, Snow. Who knows if we will be still dancing together in two months' time? This is where our lives could take different directions. I'm not sure I know how to deal with that." He takes my hand.

I never thought about that. Now I'm going to panic about being split up from Christian, Melly, and Max. They've all become so important to me.

Melly leans over the top of the chair and taps me on the shoulder. "You two are so negative. Of course we won't be split up. Everyone knows we'll be staying together. We work so well together." Melly is always so positive. I wish I could be more like her.

When we arrive at the Empire Hotel in Manhattan, which is supposedly close to the Lincoln Center, we're shown to our rooms. The first thing Melly does is run into our room and jump on one of the huge beds. We have a separate area with a couch as well. Yes, this is going to be fun! This is pure luxury.

"Oh my God! Oh my God, Snow! This is freaking amazeballs." She jumps up and down on the bed and then throws herself down flat on the bed again.

"I can't believe we're staying here. This is fantastic. I'm so nervous, Melly. This is New fucking York! This is where dreams are made or lives are shattered. Make or break!"

"Yeah, it sure is, but do you know what? You are freaking amazing. You have made *The Nutcracker* THE ballet to see. Ticket sales have sky rocketed and I overheard Patrick saying they've never had such good profits from a tour. They all love you."

We roll over and face each other. Patrick is the male judge from the auditions. He has been my number one supporter.

"Really? Do you honestly believe that?"

"I do, Snow. Really, I do! Anyway, less of the chitter chatter. We're going exploring." She kicks her feet up in the air to give herself some leverage to sit up and get off the bed. She can be so childlike sometimes.

"I want to sleep!" I whine. The journey and the party last night have worn me out.

Laughing, she comes to my side of the bed,

grabs my arm, and pulls me off it. "Get off me," I say, pulling my arm back. But she doesn't stop until I fall on the floor.

"We can sleep tonight, but now we have to do some sightseeing. We don't have a lot of time before we have to start rehearsing, so come on! Let's go look around. Max and Christian are ready; they just text me."

I groan. "Okay, let me go and freshen up first."

She lets go of me and I start to get back on the bed to sleep, but she jumps on top of me until I stand up and walk into the bathroom.

"I hate you!" I shout out to her as I slam the bathroom door. I splash some water on my face and lean on my hands to look in the mirror. "Snow, are you ready for New York?" I say to myself. I shake my head and laugh. "More like is New York ready for me?"

When I walk out of the bathroom, the two guys are waiting with Melly. "Come on then. What are you waiting for?" I say, grabbing my jacket and walking out of the room. They follow me, laughing.

"Let's go to Central Park; I've always wanted a ride on one of those horse and carts," Max says, smiling at Christian.

I love watching the two of them. I don't

know how anyone doesn't know they're a couple; they can't stop looking at or touching each other.

"So, erm, when are you going to come clean, you two?" I say, bumping Christian on the shoulder.

"We thought we would wait until the end of the tour because we don't want any bad publicity for the show."

"Why would there be bad publicity? You two are made for each other. You belong together, so tell everyone."

"We'll see," Christian says, smiling at Max.

"God, I feel like a right gooseberry," Melly says, walking off in front of us.

We find a horse and cart and climb aboard for the forty-five minute trip. The driver is really talkative and he tells us the history of the park as we go. He drops us off at the Tavern on the Green where we go to have a drink; non-alcoholic, of course. You have to be twenty-one to drink in the States, so we're underage. It's such an iconic building, and we love reading about its history while we're there. It's too busy to stay so we head off to have a look around.

"Oh my God, look at that over there!" Melly shouts, getting excited. I follow the direction she's pointing in and I see a group of guys playing some ball sport. We walk towards them to get a better view.

"They're playing baseball," Max says, smiling. "I've only ever watched baseball in *High School Musical*, but it was hot!"

We laugh at him; he can be such a girl!

Sitting down, we watch the teams pitching and running around the diamond. There are eighteen guys running around. Actually, let me rephrase that. There are eighteen really *fit* guys running around. Not fit as in go to the gym, but fit as in hot! I'm quite happy to sit and watch them. On our travels around the world, I've met a few nice guys and had a few flings, but nothing serious. How can anything be serious when we don't stay in one place long enough? I can appreciate a good-looking guy though, and right this minute, I'm looking at eighteen of them.

Melly nudges me. "Look at those guys. I could watch them for hours."

"I know. They're all hot, but there's one or two that stand out," I say, pointing to them.

Max leans forward and says, "Yeah, they're hot, but no one is a patch on Christian, I'm afraid." He reaches over and grabs Christian's hand. He doesn't care about anyone seeing them; he loves him and wants to tell the world.

We've obviously caught the attention of the baseball players as they keep looking over to us. Maybe it's because Melly is jumping up and down like a lunatic, and the fact we keep pointing at them, trying to decide who is the hottest. One or two of them even wave at us. When their game is over, they pick up their stuff and walk in our direction. Wow, they are really forward, and the closer they get, the hotter I see they are.

"Hey, did you enjoy the game? We saw you watching us," one of them says. He's really tall, blonde, and disgustingly handsome.

"Yeah, it's our first time watching baseball," Melly says, standing and walking towards him. She extends her hand to him and says, "Melly."

He smiles. "Noah." He shakes her hand. He turns to look at the rest of us.

Melly says, "Snow," pointing at me and then, "Max and Christian."

I wave, but the boys just lift their chins to say hello. He turns and introduces his friends. "Logan, Nathan, Elijah, and Ethan." I look from one to the next; they're like GQ models or something.

"Oh my God, are you guys English?" one of

them says, but I'm not really sure who it is at this stage; their names haven't sunk in yet.

"Yeah!" Melly doesn't have any problems with talking to these strangers.

"Are you on holiday here? Are you staying long?" Noah asks, taking a seat next to her.

"Yep, we are. We're here for about a month, I think." She looks at me; I don't think she wants to tell them we're here to perform. She wants them to think we're just regular holidaymakers. I'm happy with that.

"Where are you staying?" one of them says, as he sits next to me.

"The Empire Hotel." I smile at him.

He's tall as well; I think he's taller than Christian. I blush because it doesn't happen often that someone is tall enough for me. He's gorgeous. I can feel my heart getting faster as I talk to him.

"Ooh, swanky! What are your plans while you're here?" He inches closer to me.

"We want to see all the sights, of course. We've already had a horse and cart trip around the park. We'll be looking for something to do every day. Any suggestions?" I ask, fluttering my eyelashes at him.

He laughs and says, "I'm sure I can think of something for you to do while you're here."

He lifts his eyebrows up and down.

Now I really blush. He's so good-looking I don't know where to look. "I might have to pass on that one."

He laughs, like really belly laughs. "I'm Ethan, just in case you didn't catch it earlier. Snow. That's a very unusual name."

"Yeah, my mum thought it would be funny considering my colouring. It gets me a lot of attention though."

"I'm sure it does, although your beauty will catch anyone's attention first." I laugh at him. Did he really say that? "Cheesy or what?" he says, digging me in the ribs.

Max and Christian are talking to the other guys, and Noah is talking to Melly. They seem to have hit it off as well.

"I'm sure you can think of a better line than that. So, tell us what is there to do around here, as a tourist, of course," I say, turning to face him. My mouth goes dry and I'm sure I make a gulping noise. He's sitting really close and I can smell him. He smells so manly, even after all his running around.

"Well, there are all the basic tourist things to do, but one of the things I enjoy the most is Coney Island. Do you like rides?" He smiles at me like a small child in a sweet shop. I can see the excitement in his eyes. This is obviously something he really enjoys.

"Yes, I do. I think we might go to Coney Island when we get some time." Whoops, I nearly said *on a day off.*

"Give me your number, and if you want, I can take you there. It's not far and it's so much fun. It's always better when you're with someone who knows their way around the place." He takes his phone out of his pocket and starts to add in a new number.

"You just want my number, don't you? Why don't you just ask me straight?"

He laughs. "You got me, but I really would like to take you to Coney Island. I think we could have a lot of fun."

I give him my number, because, who wouldn't? He rings it to make sure I gave him the right number. "Call me," he says, after he's done something on his phone.

"God, I hope it's nothing embarrassing." I save his number and ring it. It's silent for a few seconds and I hear *Sex On Fire.* Now I'm blushing like mad. I think he's trying to tell me he likes me.

One of the guys says, "Come on. We have to go. It's eight o'clock. We need to get an early night tonight."

"Shit! I'm really sorry but we have to go. I could sit here and talk to you all night. Let me know when you're free so we can take you guys to Coney Island." He leans across and kisses me on my cheek. My heart races. Oh … My … God!

"Talk to you later, Ethan. It was great to meet you all," I say to the rest of the gang. We watch them walk away.

"They were really fun and so friendly," I say.

"Hell, they were gorgeous," Christian says, laughing.

"Yeah, they sure were," Melly adds. "Who would have known we would meet such handsome men on our first afternoon in New York? Way to go Team Nutcracker!"

We make our way back to the hotel to have some dinner as we're starving. The rest of the troupe is eating so we join them. Everyone talks about what they've done today.

My phone beeps with a text. It reminds me that I need to call home and let them know I'm okay.

"Hey Snow, it was great to meet u 2day. Don't forget Coney Island."

I smile and I'm sure I blush.

"Who's that?" Melly asks.

I look at her and blush again. "It's Ethan. You know, from earlier today."

"I remember who he is." She laughs. "So, what does he want?"

"He wants us all to go to Coney Island when we have some free time."

"Oh, yeah. That sounds great. Tell him yes!"

"I will, but we need to find out what free time we'll have. If we have a performance twice a day then we won't have much."

"Very true."

"Back at ya! I'll find out from the group when we will be free, but I would really like to go."

I sit back in my chair and listen as Melly asks what our plans are and whether anyone knows how much free time we will be getting. No one knows.

"Well … if you don't want to wait for the group, I can take u on your own."

"Thanks."

I don't know what else to say.

After dinner, we make our way back to our

room. I'm wrecked and need to sleep. We quickly unpack our bags before climbing into bed.

Just as I'm dropping off, I get a text:

"Goodnight Snow, hope I get to see u again soon."

I don't reply, but he has put a huge smile on my face.

ETHAN

"Ethan, are you still trying to get her to meet you? Can you not take a hint, man?" Noah says to me for the third time this week. "She isn't interested. Get over it. There are plenty more girls out there. You don't need to wait around for one girl who isn't going to be here long anyway.

"I know, but she's just different and she intrigues me. I feel like I need to know her. Like she's going to be important in my life."

"Oh my God, you are such a sap!" Noah laughs and pats me on the back as he walks past me.

My phone beeps with a text. I feel my heart speeding up. I hope it's her … I hope it's her … It IS her.

"Morning, just letting you know we will be free on Tuesday. Is that a problem?"

Damn! We're having an exam on Tuesday.
"Noah, what time is our exam on Tuesday?"
"Oh, she texted you, did she?" He laughs. "You're lucky, it's at ten o'clock. We should be done by one."
I text back straight away:

"We will be free from two if you want to go to Coney Island then."

I wait … and wait … it beeps again.

"Perfect! We'll meet you at Columbus Circle."

"I can't wait. C U then Snow."

"I'm guessing we're going to Coney Island on Tuesday after the exam," Noah says, smiling.
"I'm doing you a favor. I know you like her friend. What was her name?"

"Melly. It's an unusual name as well, isn't it?" He walks away to do some stretches.

"Class, can I have your attention, please?" Joan says, clapping her hands. Joan is our stretching coach. She warms us up for the grueling class that we have in half an hour. Her sessions are bad enough. I don't know how we manage the class after.

We congregate around her, but she doesn't speak until we're all standing in front of her. You can hear a pin drop. "I'm not sure if you're aware, but the Royal Ballet are here performing *The Nutcracker* in the Lincoln Center. They have been on a world tour and they are closing the tour here. We're very lucky to have secured you all a ticket to their final performance. We will be there scouting for new members for our tour which starts rehearsing in two months. As you know, we will be performing *Swan Lake,* and we'll also be doing a world tour, starting and ending here on Broadway."

"Wow, I can't wait. I love *The Nutcracker*," I say, to no one in particular. Everyone starts talking about it; there's a real buzz in class today.

Joan claps her hands to bring our attention back to class. "That's enough slacking. Take your places at the bar. Plie in first position. NOW!" And so it goes on for the next half hour. By the end of it, we're exhausted.

We get a five minute break before our next dance class. After going back to my locker and getting some water, I check my phone.

"Is it wrong I am excited and nervous about Tuesday?"

I smile at my phone, thinking about how to reply.

"Oh, no. You've got it bad. I thought you were a single guy out to have fun," Noah says, laughing as he nudges me. "You looked pussy whipped and you haven't even been on a date with her."

"Who says it's her?"

"Your face says it's her! Come on. Let's go and get killed for the next hour." He pushes away from his locker.

"No, I'm the same."

I put my phone back in my bag, but we continue texting back and forward all day during my breaks.

At the end of the day, we're exhausted, and we go to the gym to use the Jacuzzi to try and rest our muscles. This is what it's like every day. Grueling, hard work, exhausting, but I love it. I'd always wanted to be a ballet dancer since I was able to walk. I had to toughen up quickly because I was a huge target for the bullies to push around. They thought being a ballet dancer meant I was weak. They didn't realize how strong you have to be to be able to dance for hours and lift your partner in some of the moves.

I started working out as soon as I was able to, and then I was bigger than the bullies and I fought back. I've attended The American School of Ballet since I was six. The kids in my neighborhood called me all sorts of names, but I rose above them. I wasn't going to let anyone ruin my dancing dreams.

I'm impulsive, and after I leave the gym and say goodbye to Noah and the other lads, I text Snow. I can't help myself.

"Can I see you?"

I hold my breath for the five minutes it takes for her to reply.

"When?"

"Now?"

It takes her ten minutes to reply this time. My heart is in my mouth the whole time.

"Where?"

"Outside your hotel. I'm here now, but I'll wait for you. I'll take you for coffee!"

"Be right down."

I'm so excited. I'm leaning against the wall of the hotel when she walks out of the door ten minutes later. She's smiling and she looks beautiful.

"Hey, come on. Let me buy you that coffee," I say, steering her towards the coffee shop.

We move to the booth at the back of the shop, and when she slides in, I slide in opposite her. I want to look at her. "What did you do today, Snow?"

She giggles. "We went to the Empire State Building and the Statue of Liberty. I'm wrecked after all that walking. What about you? What did you do today?"

"I had classes today. It was a really tough day, and then I went to the gym with the boys. Well … we only went into the Jacuzzi." I smile, handing her a menu.

"I'm dying to use the gym at the hotel. I hear they have a lovely Jacuzzi. Oh my God, did you know they have a rooftop pool? I really want to have a go in that."

"Yeah, I know. We've been there a few times."

The waitress comes over and takes our order.

We talk for about an hour, and I know she has to get back. To be honest, I need to sleep because tomorrow is going to be even more grueling than today. We have exams to prepare for. Well, more like auditions. Each year, we have to audition for a place in the infamous troupe who tour during the summer months. I've secured a place for the last nine years, and I don't intend to let that change this year. But this year, I want it more than anything.

Snow yawns.

"Come on. Let's go," I say, sliding out of the booth. I hold out my hand for her to take so I can pull her out of her seat. She takes it and slides over to me. When I pull her upright, she crashes into my chest. I look down at her.

"Oh my God, I'm sorry." She breathes heavily. I think she's affected by me as much as I am by her.

I smile and pull her out of the coffee shop. I don't let go of her hand once we're out into the balmy night. We slowly amble our way back to her hotel and then we stand looking at each other. Neither of us wants to say goodnight or break the spell we're under.

I smile. "I ... I need to go." Her smile drops. "I'd stay with you all night if I could," I say, pulling her closer to me. "I want to kiss you so badly, but I don't know if you want me to." I stare into her eyes. It makes such a difference to be talking to a girl who is only shorter than me by an inch and not ten inches.

"I ... I want you to kiss me." She looks so scared as she looks up into my eyes. I smile and lean forward, and very gently touch my lips to hers. I get a shock and jump back. She rubs her lips with two of her fingers. "What ... what was that?"

I laugh. "I don't know, but I want to do it again." She laughs and I lean in again to kiss her. This time, I pull her close and put one of my hands around the back of her head.

When my lips touch hers, I feel the spark

again, but I kiss her deeper and deeper. I never knew a kiss could be this good.

After a few minutes, I pull away. I don't want to, but I could do this all night, and neither of us wants that to happen – yet.

I rest my forehead against hers and then cup her cheek with my hand. "You're going to be trouble, Snow. With a capital T."

"I think you might be right, Ethan." She starts laughing.

I release her and say goodnight. She walks into the hotel and then turns at the last minute to wave goodbye before she gets into the lift. I smile and walk back home. She feels different to any of the other girls I've been out with. Maybe she's 'the one'. I laugh to myself; that is a load of baloney – something always happens and nothing lasts forever. Just look at Mum and Dad. They loved each other so much, but they were so possessive that it became toxic. I never want to be in that situation, ever.

Five

THREE YEARS LATER

SNOW

The crowd is silent as I dance the last step in *Swan Lake*. It's such a powerful dance that I can feel the tears forming in my eyes. The applause starts and the curtains go down. I slump to the floor, exhausted. Ethan comes over to help me up

"Babe, you were amazing. God, I love you!" He pulls me to him to give me support and he helps me off the stage. I sit and take some sips of my water while we wait for the curtain to go up so we can all go out for our curtain call. We receive a standing ovation, and each and every time we get one of those, it makes me want to cry. I can't tell you how much it moves me that people are so invested emotionally in our dance that they feel they can stand and clap for us. We hold hands, walk to the front of the stage, Ethan bows, and I curtsy. He lets go of my hand then walks to the left of the stage and I walk to the front. The rest of the troupe joins us, and then we leave the stage. The curtain rises once more and we all go out and bow together. This happens another three times, and then that is enough. We leave the sides of the stage and go back to our dressing room.

Once inside, Ethan and I flop down on the sofa. We're both exhausted but exhilarated from being on stage. Three years ago, we met and started dating, then when he came to watch *The Nutcracker*, we realised we have the same love of ballet. It wasn't something he had mentioned to me because he had had difficulties with girls finding out he was a ballet dancer before, but when we realised this, we knew that us meeting was destiny. We were soul mates, meant to be together forever.

Melly comes in and hugs me and then says, "Right guys, this is our last night here in Copenhagen, so let's go out and party. Let's celebrate! We're going to Stockholm tomorrow for three nights and then onto London. I can't wait to go home. It's been a long time!" After both of us were approached by The New York Ballet Company after seeing us perform in *The Nutcracker*, we went home for two months to get everything in order before we went back to New York to start rehearsing with them for their tour. We were lucky that they wanted both of us to dance with them. We've been on the move ever since. I can't wait to see my family and introduce them to Ethan.

"Great idea. Give us twenty minutes. We need to shower first." I smile, and having stood up from the couch, I push her out of the door.

Ethan smiles at me. "A shower, huh?" He stands as well, and starts to stalk towards me. "Does that mean we can shower together? I love it best when we shower together ... and it's twice as quick."

"No it's not, it usually takes longer, but if you're quick to get undressed, then yeah, we can shower together."

By the time I've finished my sentence, he's in front of me with no clothes on. I never tire of looking at his body. He walks towards me and starts to help me out of my tutu, then he kneels in front of me and unlaces my ballet shoes, and carefully removes them. He gently massages my feet as he knows how sore they get. After taking my tights off, he slowly drags me to the shower in our dressing room. Turning the water to warm, he pulls me in under the cascading water and hugs me for a couple of minutes. I can feel his cock come to life, and it nudges against me. I smile. He kisses me intensely and I wrap my arms around him and feel his hard muscles and his tight arse.

He takes the shower crème, and after pouring it into his hand, he rubs it in his hands before rubbing them all over my body. It feels so good, and I notice he spends more time on my breasts, especially my nipples. He pulls them and then leans down and puts one of them into his mouth.

I moan. "God, Ethan, we don't have …" I don't get to finish what I'm saying before he plunges a finger inside me.

He chuckles and releases my nipple, kisses his way up to my mouth, and sticks his tongue into my mouth. I love when he kisses me; it does so many things to me, making me lose myself in everything that is Ethan. I forget everything that's going on in my life, and all my problems fade away.

It's my turn to wash him. He still has his fingers inside me and it's making me lose my mind; I can't concentrate on cleaning him. I love running my hands down his washboard stomach to the 'V' that runs down to the grand prize. I grab his cock and start to clean it. Well, that's what I tell myself.

He groans and then takes his fingers out of me and turns me around so my back is facing him. He pushes me so my hands are spread on the wall. He bends his knees and takes his cock in his hand. "Are you ready for me, Snow? I need to be inside you right now and I can't wait."

"I'm always ready for you, Ethan. Fuck me hard!"

He does exactly what I ask and he takes me hard … really hard. It's over in a short time but we're both exhausted afterwards. We clean each other before leaving the shower and getting ready for the party.

Walking out to the back door of the theatre, we find Melly is waiting for us. "What took you so long, guys?" She looks at us. "Actually, don't tell me. I already know. We are going to HIVE tonight. It's going to be packed but we're going to get hammered and have loads of fun!"

Melly likes to party much more than I do, but tonight is special. It's the end of our time here in Copenhagen, and like every city we've been in, we always party on the last night.

Once we're inside the club, we do shots of Hot Nuts. It's Fireball and hazelnut liquor, and it is de...lic...ious! Just don't have too many of them because it's not much fun!

ONE WEEK LATER

ETHAN

We've just arrived in London and are rehearsing in The Royal Opera House. This building is amazing. It's so old and beautiful, and when you stand on the stage, you can feel the hundreds of years of performances in the air. There have been so many performances that have gone before us in the three hundred years that this building has been used.

This building has been burnt to the ground a few times, but it keeps rising from the ashes like a phoenix, and it proves the determination of all its performances and performers.

Opening night is tomorrow, so we've been really busy, but this evening, I'm going to Snow's house to meet her parents. This is really big for me. I never wanted to be that far into a relationship that I had to meet the family. Snow is different, though. My relationship with her just happens. It's not hard to be with her; it's easy and feels perfect. I love her like I've never loved anyone before. We're meant to be together forever. I know my parents were consumed with each other but we're not the same as they were. I see that now. I don't ever want to change the way we are.

After we finish rehearsing, which is seriously grueling, we're back in the hotel room, getting ready for tonight. Snow has stayed with me in the hotel rather than staying at her parents' because we have to be at rehearsals early and we stay late. Well, that's what we've told her parents.

"Are you ready, Ethan?" Snow is pacing in the bedroom while I finish getting ready in the bathroom.

I walk out and reach for my jacket. "Yeah. I'm ready now." I'm not sure how I feel about meeting her parents, but I want to be a part of her life forever, so I need to meet them. "Do you think they'll like me?" I'm a little bit nervous.

She rushes over to me and takes my hands. "Ethan, stop worrying. They will love you. You're amazing. Come on. Let's get it out of the way and then we can go out for a few drinks with Melly and Noah." She reaches up and kisses me. "I love you. You know that, don't you?"

"I know you do. I love you more!" When she smiles at me like that, I know everything is going to be fine. Her parents are going to like me and we ARE going to be happy.

SNOW

I'm really nervous about bringing Ethan to meet my parents. They're open minded and liberal, which is great, but I'm still worried about how they will react when they see Ethan. I've never brought a white boy back to the house before. Actually, I've never dated a white boy before. I don't really think of his colour. I love him for being him. Obviously, they know, but I'm still worried. Hopefully everything will go to plan and it will all be a distant memory at the end of the night.

"Come on then. Let's go feed you to the lions," I say, smiling up at him.

When the taxi drops us outside my parents' house, Ethan grabs hold of me and kisses me. "Just for luck," he says. Smiling, I take his hand, and we walk into the house.

The house is a normal semi-detached house. You walk in the front door, and in the hall there is a set of stairs on one side of the hall and a wall and a door into the lounge on the other. We walk in there and Mum and Dad are standing, waiting for us.

"Oh my God, Snow. You look great. I can't believe it's been so long since we saw you. We missed you, you know?" Mum walks over and hugs me, and Dad follows behind her.

"Mum, Dad, this is Ethan." I take his hand, and he holds up his free hand so he can shake hands with my parents.

"Don't be so formal; give us a hug," Mum says, grabbing him from me and hugging him. "It's so good to meet you! We've heard so much about you."

"It's good to meet you too," he says, slightly muffled as she is still hugging him tight.

When she lets go, he holds his hand out to my dad and shakes his hand. "It's good to meet you too, sir," he says.

"The feeling's mutual," Dad says.

We go through to the dining room and I see Mum has laid the table as if it's Christmas; she has gone all out. Bless her, she must be as nervous as Ethan is.

Everything goes well, and after dinner, Dad and Ethan take the dishes into the kitchen then sit in the lounge. Mum and I wash the dishes and put them away.

"He's really nice, Snow! I like him. I think your Dad does too. I can definitely see what you see in him."

"I'm so happy, Mum. He makes me so happy. When you're a ballet dancer, it's so hard to have a relationship because of the travelling and the schedules. You know yourself how hard it is." Mum was a ballet dancer when she met my dad. He is not a dancer and it was really hard to keep their relationship going. When he asked her to marry him, she immediately left her beloved ballet dancing because he had come to mean more to her than her dancing. I can't see how she could feel like that. What would I do if Ethan wasn't a dancer? I just don't know.

We stay for a few hours, and then we leave to go and meet Melly. "Thanks for dinner, Mum. It was delicious. You're coming to opening night, aren't you? I have tickets left for you."

"Of course we are. We wouldn't miss it for the world." She hugs me. "I love you, Snow."

"Love you too."

Dad hugs me and says the same.

We get into the waiting taxi and go to the pub, where Melly, Noah, Max, and the other guys are waiting for us.

Seven

NEW YORK

TWO YEARS LATER

SNOW

I've lost count of the number of times I've danced on this stage in the Lincoln Centre, but for some reason, it's the one stage that always has the power to reduce me to tears. It is really iconic; it moves me so much.

The lights go off … The audience is silent … The music starts off softly and I move en pointe in small, fluid movements out onto the stage. That's 'on the tips of my toes' for those of you who haven't danced ballet. This is my favourite part of the whole performance; the feeling of entering a stage with a captive audience who are waiting for me to shine.

It's still in darkness, and as I move to the middle of the stage, moving my arms up and down like the swan that I am, I get excited knowing that the light is going to shine on me and I'm going to continue en pointe and turn around to face the audience.

My feet will hurt like a bitch, they always do after this part of the dance, but I have to just dance through the pain. I can bathe them later, when I'm resting. Ethan will massage them for me; he is fantastic at massaging my feet while I massage his.

It is such an emotional dance; I have to make sure my emotions show on my face as well as in my dancing. 'The Dying Swan' is my pièce de résistance. I love dancing in *Swan Lake* and have been the main swan for the last three years. I dance with the New York Ballet, and that's where I met Ethan.

Ethan is the love of my life. He is a ballet dancer as well, and he is so sexy, kind, and considerate. We travel around the world dancing in ballets and living our lives in some of the most prestigious hotels and cities around the globe.

I met Ethan when I had just arrived in New York, and we hit it off immediately. I am now living the dream!

Nothing could ever be better than this moment. The dance is coming to an end. I'm down on the stage, waving my arms about as the swan dies. The lights go out and the audience goes wild. I can see a standing ovation. This is for me! This is the best feeling in the world ... This moment, right now!

As the curtain goes down, I stand and walk off the stage. Seeing Ethan in the wings, I collapse into his arms. The dance is soul consuming and has taken every last bit of emotion out of me.

"You were amazing, babe. I love you." He holds me tight and whispers into my ear.

"Thank ... thank you." I'm out of breath. "I love you too. Now go and knock them dead." He kisses me quickly and then starts to move towards the stage. I watch for as long as I can before I have to leave the wings.

After we have bowed and curtsied on the final curtain, we go to our dressing room and sit on the couch. It always takes us about half an hour to come down from the adrenaline buzz before we can get changed and leave the theatre. There is a bottle of champagne waiting for us, and Ethan opens it with a flourish.

Sitting and sipping our champagne, Ethan says, "I love life right now, Snow. We have an amazing life. I love you more than anyone I've ever known. Will you marry me?"

Wow, did he just propose to me? "Oh my God, Ethan! Yes!" I almost scream in his face. He places a ring on my finger. I didn't even know he was holding it up to me. I kiss him and then start jumping all over the place.

The dressing room door opens and Melly runs in. "What's going on?"

"Ethan proposed. I said yes."

She starts screaming too. "Snow. Snow!" She's not jumping up and down like I thought she would. She looks worried.

"I know! It's so fantastic! I can't wait to ring my mum and tell her. She'll be so excited!" I say, moving towards her for a hug.

"No, Snow ..." she says, pointing to the robe I'm wearing.

Looking down, I see there's blood running down my legs. "What's happening to me?" I start screaming and then I pass out.

ETHAN

"Quick, Melly, call an ambulance." I have to practically push her out the door. I lift Snow up and lay her on the couch where we were sitting when I proposed.

"Snow, baby, wake up. Please! What's wrong with you?" I get a towel and wrap it around her so no one can see whatever is happening to her. All sorts of things are going around my head. Cancer … Tumor … Whatever it is, we will go through it together. There is no other way. I wipe her brow and kiss her. "Baby, please."

Melly runs in. "The ambulance will be here in four minutes; they will look after her. Ethan, what's going on?"

"I don't know, Melly! She was fine. I proposed, and when she put the ring on, you came in. I know as much as you do!"

"We need to ring her parents."

"We can't until we know what's going on. They're in London. They aren't due over here for another week." She nods in agreement. I bow my head. "Melly, I'm scared. What if she's really sick? What will we do?"

"Come on, Ethan. You need to be strong for her. She will be fine, I promise." She touches me on my shoulder and I put my hand over hers for comfort.

The door opens with a thud and two paramedics walk through. "Right, give us some space and tell us what happened."

I don't want to leave her, but they need the space to get closer to her. They start taking their observations.

"She ... she was really happy. She jumped up and down and then the blood just started running down her leg. We don't even know where it's coming from."

We stand and watch what they're doing. They're checking her temperature, her pulse, her breathing.

"Everything looks to be okay. We need to take her to the hospital to find out the cause of the bleeding. Is there a chance she could be pregnant, sir?" he asks as he looks at me.

I pale. "No ... no way. She's on birth control. She always has been. No ... no way!" I can feel myself panicking.

"That's okay. You understand we have to ask, especially if we have to do any x-rays." He turns back to face Snow. She's getting paler and paler by the second.

Melly touches me on the arm and nods her head to the corner of the room. I follow her. "Ethan. If I had to bet money on it, I would say she's having a miscarriage. Are you absolutely sure she isn't pregnant?"

I keep shaking my head. "No! We're never having kids; we agreed that we don't want kids. Our dancing is the most important thing to me in the world after her. Neither of us wants to give it up, EVER!" I can feel my world starting to fall apart. We have spent so long building our perfect life around dancing that there isn't room for anything else. We don't want anything else in our life.

"Okay, calm down. I was only asking. She's so good with all the kids that I thought you might have changed your mind or something."

"No, never!" I'm adamant on that one.

"Sorry to interrupt, but we need to get her out of here. We've hooked her up to some fluids to help her, but we need to get some blood for her. She's still losing it and we need to get to the hospital." The second paramedic must have got a gurney because Snow is laying on it and they're starting to wheel her out of the room to the ambulance. I follow behind them, worried about her. Melly is right behind me; she looks scared too.

When we get to the hospital, they put Snow straight into a cubicle and ask us to leave while they assess her. Melly and I sit outside on these horrible, hard chairs. We sit there for what seems like hours, but it's probably only one.

A doctor comes out. "Who are you to Snow?"

"I'm … I'm her fiancé."

"I'm her best friend. We come from London, but we're dancing over here," Melly says with a shaky voice.

"Okay, you can come in and see her. She's still not conscious. We're keeping her hydrated with fluids and we're considering a blood transfusion, but we need someone to sign on her behalf as she can't do it herself. Come in and see her first and then we can talk." He opens the curtain for us to go inside.

I can feel the tears forming in my eyes. She is laid on the table, with a white sheet covering her up to her chest. She looks like she's fast asleep, but she looks different. She looks so pale. Her usual milk chocolate skin has taken a grey pallor and she just doesn't look right. She doesn't look like Snow.

"Oh my God, Ethan. She looks dead." She catches her breath and I can hear her sobbing.

"She looks like Snow White laid out waiting for Prince Charming to come and rescue her. Maybe if I kiss her she might come back to us." I know I'm clutching at straws, but anything is worth the chance. I lean over and rub her head then gently kiss her lips. Nothing. Nothing happens. I try again. I look at Melly. "Why's it not working? Why is she not waking for me?"

She comes over and touches me to try and calm me down. I step away from the bed and flop into the chair.

"Ethan, they are doing everything they can. I think I need to go and ring her parents. They would want to know what's going on." I ignore her as she walks out of the cubicle to go make that dreaded call. I know I should ring them, but I don't want to leave her. I don't know what to say to them.

An hour later, the doctor comes back in. "Have you thought any more about signing the form for a blood transfusion? We really believe she needs it."

"Yeah, go ahead. Do it. Do whatever it takes." I bow my head again. I just need her to get better. I need my Snow back.

The doctors work quickly to set up the transfusion and then they leave us alone again. At some stage, Melly comes back in, but she doesn't say anything. I can see she's been crying though. It must have been so hard to make that call.

One of the nurses comes back in with a small machine and sets it up in the corner then leaves again. There are a few people coming and going for a short period of time. Finally, the doctor comes back in with a small, stout lady, who sits at the small machine. She smiles at me and looks at the screen.

The doctor says, "We have had some results of some of the tests that we performed when she first came in."

I stand and walk to the bed, where I take Snow's hand. "Yes? And?" Melly has stood beside me and takes my other hand.

"Well, the good news is that Snow is pregnant!" he says with a smile.

"What? How?" I let go of her hand and move out of Melly's grasp. I sit back down in the chair and put my head in my hands. I shake my head. "No!"

"I thought you would be happy. However, with the amount of blood that she has lost, we're certain that she is having a miscarriage. Mary over here is the sonographer and she is going to check to see if there is still a heartbeat or not." He nods his head to Mary. "Go ahead."

Mary drags her chair so that she's closer to Snow. She rolls down the sheet and folds it down. Snow is laying there with her stomach on show. Mary rubs some jello like substance around on her belly and then she gets the probe and presses down hard. It looks like it could be sore, but Snow doesn't even flinch. We all hold our breath and the room is silent.

So quiet …

Silent …

Mary is frowning at the screen.

"What is it? What do you see?" Melly shouts at her.

Mary looks at the doctor and he walks over to her and she points at something on the screen.

Silence …

Then … beep, beep, beep, beep.

Melly starts crying. "Oh my God, Ethan!"

"What? What?"

Mary smiles. "There it is. You can hear it if you're quiet."

"WHAT?!"

No one is saying anything.

Beep, beep, beep, beep. It's getting louder and faster. She looks at me. "Congratulations, Ethan. You're going to be a dad! She didn't lose the baby!"

I don't know what to say. I stand up. "I don't want a child. We agreed we wouldn't have children. How did she let this happen?" I storm out of the room. I can't deal with this.

Was she tricking me? Lying to me even?

I can hear Melly calling after me. "Ethan, stop! Don't be so selfish! Stay and be here when she wakes. She'll want to talk to you. You are the one she'll want to see, not me!"

"Sorry, Melly. I need to go get my head together. I'll be back in a while."

I walk out of the hospital into the cold, windy night. I start to walk home. I don't care that it's cold. I have to think about what has happened today. How has my life fallen apart so quickly? I have a lot of texts on my phone but I ignore them and ring Noah.

"Hey, can you meet me?"

"Yeah, sure. Is Snow okay? I heard what happened at the theatre."

"I'll tell you when I see you. Can you meet me at the Fidel's Pub?"

"Yeah. Are you sure she's okay?"

"Just meet me there. I'm on my way." I hang up the phone.

I can't believe this is happening to me. How did she get pregnant? Why did she get pregnant? We didn't have this in our plan, so why?

Eight

LONDON

FIVE YEARS LATER

SNOW

"Mummy, Mummy! Show me again. I want to dance like you!" Gracie is pulling on my leg, trying to move me into the middle of the room. She likes it when I show her my dance moves. I don't like dancing anymore; it brings back so many memories I want to try and forget. But she won't give up until I do a pas de chat.

I let her move me into the centre of the lounge. "Mummy, do the jump thing. What's it called again? A pa ... pa ... I can't say it.

Mummy, you say it so beautiful!"

"It's a pas de chat, Gracie. If you want to do ballet dancing then you need to learn how to say the words as well as do the steps." I hold her hand and she stands next to me. "Okay, so we stand in first position, hold out our right arm, bend our left arm so that your hand is at your waist. Point your fingers like this ..." I show her how to hold her fingers. "Watch me, Gracie, then copy me, okay?"

She smiles at me while she holds her hands still.

"Bend your left knee, point your toes, and then jump at the same time. When you're in the air, bend the right knee and kick them and kick your bum. Then straighten the right knee and bring the left one down. So it's like a pair of scissors. Now watch me!" She steps back and watches me do the perfect pas de chat. She claps her little hands as she's watching me. Once you've mastered it, you never forget it. I can feel the tears forming once again. God, I need to grow a pair of balls and suck it up!

"Mummy, you're so beautiful. I want to do it. I want to do it." She's jumping up and down. I smile at her and she moves to the centre of the room. I move back to watch her. She holds her hands the way I told her and then she tries to jump. It doesn't go well, so she tries again. After about five tries she manages to do a passable pas de chat. I clap my hands like she did for me.

"Gracie, you are amazing! You look so beautiful!" She runs up to me and throws herself at me. While we're hugging, my phone starts ringing. I put her down and take out my phone. I smile when I see it's Spencer. I met him about six months ago on one of my very rare nights out. He's really different. He takes care of me and is very gentle and loving. He's thoughtful and he seems to really like me. "I have to get this, sweetheart. I'll be right back! Keep practising and I'll watch you when I get back."

She goes back to practicing her new dance move.

"Hi."

"Hey, babe. How's things?"

"I'm just teaching Gracie some moves. She's getting better all the time."

He has always known about Gracie. I didn't want to go out with anyone, but Mum told me

I need to think about myself for a change.

"Well, if she's anything like her graceful mum then I bet she is beautiful!"

"Flattery gets you a long way, Spence."

"That's what I'm hoping"

I can hear the smile in his voice. He has a gorgeous smile. He is dark-haired, tanned, and he has a dimple in his cheek, so when he smiles, I just want to run my tongue along his dimple. I shake my head. Why are my thoughts taking me down that road?

"Well, you never know."

"We're going slightly off track here, but I was hoping you would come out and meet me tonight. I want to show you where I work. I want you to meet my friends."

Oh my God. This is epic, especially for me. I'm not sure I'm ready for a relationship like that. I know if I tell Mum, she'll tell me to go for it. So what's holding me back? Gracie is, but it's not her fault. I just don't want to get serious about someone and then she has to meet them and then, if we finish, she will be disappointed. I shake my head to stop being so negative.

"I'll have to check Mum can look after Gracie and then let you know. Is that okay?"

"Go and ask her now. I know you … you'll come up with an excuse otherwise!" He laughs. He knows me already.

"Okay … hang on!"

I walk into the kitchen where Mum is cooking dinner.

"Mum, can you look after Gracie tonight?" I nod towards the phone and mouth at her, *'I've got Spencer on the phone.'*

"Of course I can, Snow. You go and have some fun." Then she takes the phone and says, "Thank you, Spencer," before handing it back to me.

I laugh, and when I put the phone to my ear, he is laughing too.

"I guess that means I'm free tonight. What's the plan?"

"I'll collect you at eight. Is that alright?"

"Sure. See you then!"

"Can't wait to see you. You'll love my friends."

"I hope they like me."

"Of course they will. I know for sure they will. See you later, babe."

We both hang up. I stand there looking at my phone for a minute, with a smile on my face. I'm nervous and excited at the same time.

Mum walks up behind me. "Why don't you go and take a bath and relax for a while? Gracie is fine with me."

I turn and smile. "Thanks, Mum." I kiss her on the cheek and go upstairs.

After I've run the bath, I slowly sink into the hot, bubbly water. It's nice to have some time to think. I never have enough time to think these days. For the last few years, I've shied away from thinking too much. It leads me down a dark path that I don't want to go down.

I can't help but think back over the last five

years and how my life has drastically changed. I went from an in demand prima ballerina to a single parent of a beautiful baby girl. How your life can change in the blink of an eye. I try not to think of it because it makes me cry, and I don't want to cry.

Since I've met Spencer, my life has changed for the better. He likes me for who I am and not what I should be. He hasn't met Gracie yet, but if things go well tonight, then that would be the next chapter for me.

My phone rings when I'm lying there thinking of Spencer. I look at the screen and see a withheld number. I ignore it. I keep getting calls from a withheld number and when I answer, no one answers me back. It freaks me out a little bit. I used to think it might be Ethan looking for me, but it didn't take long for me to realise that that part of my life was well and truly closed off.

After I get out of the bath, I get dressed to go out. I'm not sure where we're going and I know he works in a club, so I dress up. I never get the chance these days and I know I still have a good figure, so I wear a tight dress to enhance my natural curves. I still have my dancer's body, so I'm not afraid to show it off.

I go downstairs to find Mum sitting in the

kitchen, feeding Gracie. "Hey, Mummy. You look really pretty tonight," Gracie says, looking up at me for a minute before concentrating on her pancakes.

"Yeah, you look really nice, Snow. I can see a sparkle back in your eyes," Mum says.

"Thanks, Mum." I lean down and kiss her on the cheek.

I get a text to say Spencer is outside. "Right, guys. I'm off."

"Have fun," Mum says.

I lean over and kiss Gracie. "Love you, button!"

"Love you too, Mummy. Have fun." I smile when she tries to copy her nanny.

I walk out of the house and Spence is leaning up against his car, waiting for me. He really is sex on legs. He smiles, takes my hand, and pulls me in close. "God, I missed you." He kisses me on the lips.

I squirm a little, just in case Gracie is watching.

"No one's watching, babe. Just me and you." He kisses me again.

I relax into his kiss. It sends shockwaves throughout my whole body and makes me feel like I'm melting all over him.

His voice is gruff. "We better get in the car and go or I might just do something that will make your mum's eyes pop out!" He lets me go.

I laugh. Part of me wants him to do that, and part of me is nervous. We haven't had sex yet. We've dated and been out, but I've avoided situations where it's just the two of us in an environment which will lead to sexual advances. It's not that I don't want him … I really do. I'm just scared. What if I'm not good enough? What if I don't satisfy him? I've only ever slept with Ethan so I have no way of telling whether I'm good or not.

He opens the door for me to slide in and then he goes round to his side of the car and climbs in. Smiling at me once again, he then drives to the other side of town. "Do you mind if I leave the car here tonight? I want to have a few drinks on our own and then we can go to the club to meet everyone."

"Yeah, that's fine. Will your car be okay, here?" I look around and all I can see are duplexes, and this is a square where all the cars are parked.

He laughs. "This is where I live, babe. Do you want to come in and have a look around?"

My eyes search for an escape route. I don't

know if I'm ready to take this to the next level …

"I only want to show you around. I'm not going to jump on you."

I relax.

"Not that I don't want to, but I respect you more than that, babe. Anyway, I want us to have a great night, so me seducing you before we go out would not do us any favours."

I smile and then follow him into his duplex. I realise that I DO want him to seduce me. I need someone to think of me as a woman and not a mum.

Inside is gorgeous; very unexpected. The door opens downstairs and he tells me that is where the spare bedrooms and the utility room are. He takes my hand and leads me upstairs where the hallway opens out to an open plan lounge, dining room, and kitchen. It is huge and gorgeous.

"My bedroom is on the next floor. Do you want to see that too?" he asks hesitantly.

"Of course. I want the full guided tour." I gulp. This is awkward. I want to look around, but I don't know if I want to be in his bedroom. I feel like a teenager all over again. My hands are getting clammy.

He still has hold of my hand so he takes me

and leads me upstairs once again, to his bedroom.

"This is your bedroom?" I ask incredulously.

I let go of his hand and walk around the open space. His bedroom is the full floor. He has a couch with a TV on the wall as well as a king-size bed. He has a walk-in wardrobe and his en-suite is huge. The bath would hold about four people, I reckon.

He's smiling at me when I've finished my tour. "Do you like it?"

"Oh my God, Spencer. It's amazing, I love it." He has huge windows and then he has skylights which flood the whole room in light. "I bet it's beautiful when the sun is shining."

"It gets really hot in here when the sun shines, but yes, it is gorgeous." He walks up behind me and wraps his arms around my waist so that they're clasped together at the front. He nuzzles into my neck. "You smell gorgeous." We just stand there, both in our own worlds. He eventually pulls away and takes my hand. "Come on. We need to get out of here before I break the promise I made to you earlier."

I chuckle to myself. I think, deep down, I wanted him to break his promise.

We leave and walk to a small tapas bar down the road and have some tapas and white wine. He orders Villa Maria; he knows it's my favourite. We chat about what we've been up to since we last met up.

"Tell me about your friends, Spence. Who am I going to meet tonight? I'm really nervous."

He reaches across the table. "Don't be nervous, babe. They will love you. I know they will." He takes a drink of his wine and says, "You know I work in a club, right?" I nod and he continues. "You've never asked me about the club, but it's called Whiskey Sour. Have you heard of it?"

I shake my head. "Listen, Spence, I don't go out. You know that. I was lucky that the first time I went out in ages, I met you. Other than that, I don't really get out."

He smiles at me. "Well, Whiskey Sour is a burlesque club ..." He stops talking and watches my face. I don't show any emotion. Dancing is an art form, whatever shape it takes. "Whiskey owns the club, and she went through a lot in her life before she ended up with the club. You will love her. I just know she will love you too. Jeannie and Dee Dee are her best friends, and they work in the club too.

Sawyer is Whiskey's husband, and he owned the club before he gave it to Whiskey. His best friend, Stig, works the door. He looks after the memberships and makes sure no one gets out of hand."

"I've never been to a club like that. This is going to be a great night!"

"It sure is, babe, and I've got the night off, so it will be even more fun!"

"Come on then. Let's get out of here and go check it out." I smile and down the last of the wine.

After paying for the meal and drinks, we walk outside and he wraps his arm around my shoulder and brings me in close. I look up at him and he kisses me. God, I love his kisses. I never thought I would kiss another man in my life, and yet here I am, kissing the most handsome man ever. My phone rings and I pull it out of my pocket, just in case it's Mum ringing about Gracie. It's the unknown number. I ignore it and put it back in my pocket while it's still ringing.

"Who's that? Why are you not answering it?" He holds his hand out for me to give him my phone, he wants to look at it, but when I hand it over he has a quick look through.

"I keep getting these calls from an unknown

number and then, when I speak, they hang up. So now I don't even bother answering."

"I don't like the sound of that. I can get someone to look into that for you if it bothers you a lot."

"It's fine. Just a nuisance caller. Where were we? I think you were kissing me … can we just get back to that?"

He smiles and kisses me again.

When he pulls away, I know he's reluctant, but at the same time, he wants me to meet his friends. We walk to the club, and when we're outside, I can't believe this is a burlesque club. It's very inconspicuous and not brash like I expected. I suppose I was thinking along the lines of *The Birdcage* in the movie with Robin Williams.

"Are you ready?" he asks.

I nod. "Yes. Let's go have some fun."

When he opens the door, the first thing I see is a set of stairs. As we walk down them, the door closes behind us and it's really dark. I hold onto the banister on my way down. When we get to the bottom, there is a huge man watching us. When he sees it's, Spencer, he grins and pulls him into a man hug.

"Spence, what are you doing here on your night off? Couldn't stay away from us, hey?"

"I missed you, big guy!" Spence says, smiling. He takes my hand and says, "This is Snow. Snow, this is Stig."

Stig gives me the once over and smiles. "You weren't joking when you said she was beautiful." He pulls me into a hug and then says, "I'm Stig, and I make sure there's no trouble in this joint. You're not going to be trouble, are you, pretty lady?"

I laugh. "No, I won't be any trouble. You won't even know I'm here."

He looks at Spence. "Yes, I like this lady. She can come again. Now, go off and enjoy yourselves, and make sure you hang around at the end for the signature!" I don't know what that means, but it sounds intriguing.

I follow Spence as he opens the door into the club. Once those doors are open, it's like stepping into another world. I stop and stare. The club is full, the music is loud, and the girl who is dancing is mesmerising.

I can't help but stare. I feel Spence behind me, and he whispers into my ear. "That's Jeannie. She's Stig's wife. She dances classical burlesque." I watch her and she is really beautiful. I never thought the dancing would be like this.

"Come on. Let's go to the bar." He takes my

hand and leads the way. He keeps stopping and saying hello to people on the way.

When we get to the bar, he asks me what I want to drink. "A glass of wine, please."

He nods and leaves me to watch the stage while he orders my drink. Jeannie has lost some of her clothes; I don't know how that happened as I've been watching her as she dances. How the hell did she do that?

Spence hands me a drink. I don't take my eyes off the stage. "Spence, is it wrong that this is turning me on?"

He laughs. "Not at all, babe. As a customer, that is exactly what we want you to feel. As my girlfriend, I'd rather I turn you on." He pulls me backwards so my back is against his chest. He wraps his hands around me and pulls me back so I can feel his body up against mine. He keeps his hands over my stomach and grinds his hips into mine. It makes me moan.

I laugh. "Well, that goes without saying." I push my arse back so I can feel his hard cock pushing against my cheeks.

He laughs too. "You better stop that or we won't be watching the girls for much longer."

The stage goes dark, and all of sudden, Jeannie is gone. I feel like I've been hypnotised, and as soon as the lights went out, it's like the connection was cut. I turn in his arms and lean against his chest. "Thank you for bringing me here. She was amazing." I reach up and put my hands behind his neck and bring him closer to me so I can kiss him. His hands reach down and cup my arse. We both moan and he pulls away first.

"I'm so lucky," he says.

"No. I'm the lucky one," I say, turning in his arms to watch more dancing.

Over the next hour or so, I watch the other dancers with excitement. All the girls have a different style. Some take off their clothes, some don't. It's not what I expected at all. It's exhilarating.

I've had quite a few drinks and I feel relaxed for the first time in a while. Mum had text me earlier to tell me to stay out as long as I want, and that she will take Gracie to pre-school in the morning so I can have a lie-in.

When the club starts emptying out, I drink my drink quickly. "What did you do that for?" Spencer asks. "The night is just beginning." I'm confused, but then the dancers come out one by one and sit at the bar. He introduces me to them all. Dee Dee, Jeannie, Sissy, Baby, and Sage.

Stig comes over when all the customers are

gone. "Spencer, get behind the bar, mate, and do your thing!"

"I'll be back in a minute, babe." He leans down and kisses my cheek, then he leaves me and walks around the other side of the bar. As he is making cocktails, a woman with short blonde hair walks up to our table, with a very distinguished man beside her.

"You must be Snow. We've heard so much about you. I'm Whiskey," she says, holding out her hand for me to shake.

"Hi." I shake her hand. "I've had so much fun tonight. You ladies are amazing. I loved the whole tease element, and it's great that you all have different dancing styles." It reminds me of when I came off stage, but I let it wash over me.

"I hear you're a pretty good dancer yourself," Whiskey says, and I look directly at Spencer. He shrugs his shoulders and grins at me.

"Yeah, I suppose I was, but nothing like you guys. I'm a ballerina. Sorry, I *was* a ballerina."

"Once a dancer, always a dancer!" she says, and rubs my arm. "Come on, Spence! Where are these drinks?"

He has made a different drink for each girl. He hands me one too. "It's a Sex on a

Snowbank," he says, chuckling to himself.

I laugh. The girls hold their drinks in the air and say, "To Whiskey Sour," so I do the same. Spencer, Stig, and the other guy do too.

Spencer comes around to my side of the bar and sits down next to me. "My drink is gorgeous, Spence. I love the name of it too."

He laughs. "I thought you might."

We stay for another hour and then we need to leave. It's really late and I haven't stayed out this late in a long time.

Everyone says goodbye to us and Stig makes sure we get a taxi outside.

Snuggling in the back of the taxi, I say, "I had a great night tonight, Spence. Thank you for bringing me. I loved your friends and the club is amazing."

"They loved you too," he says, pulling me close.

I lean into him. "I don't want this night to end. Can I stay with you tonight?" I don't know where that came from, but he has made me feel so special tonight that I know I want to stay with him and let him hold me all night.

"Hell yeah you can." He kisses me on the cheek and then tells the taxi driver to go to his house.

I'm ready to let him further into my life. He

really cares for me. He just better not break my heart like Ethan did.

MORNING AFTER

SNOW

The sun is streaming in and wakes me up. I roll over and pull the covers up over my head. When I do, I hear a chuckle.

I open my eyes with a start and see Spencer looking at me. What the fuck?

"Morning, babe. How's your head?"

"Oh God! What happened last night? Was I really drunk?"

"No, but you were really tired. You asked to come back and then when we were making out, you fell asleep. Sorry if I bored you." He laughs.

"I'm so sorry! I don't get out often and it was late!" I'm mortified. I can't believe I fell asleep on him.

"It's fine. Now, stay in bed. I'm off to bring you coffee." He leans over and kisses me and then climbs out of the bed. OH ... MY ... GOD! His body is amazing. How could I fall asleep with that body next to me?

I wait until he's out of the door and then I jump up and run into his en-suite. I do a wee and then find his toothpaste, put some on my finger, and brush my teeth using my finger. I run my fingers through my hair and then jump back into the bed. I giggle to myself. I'm hoping he brings me more than coffee in bed.

When he walks in, I don't think I've ever seen someone as beautiful as him. He has a six pack with that delectable 'V' that everyone talks about. It's like the pathway to heaven.

"What are you thinking about, Snow? I think I see you blushing." He hands me the coffee and then gets into the other side of the bed.

"I was wondering where that ..." I point to his stomach "is going."

He laughs. "Do you want to find out? You're more than welcome, babe." He puts his coffee down and pulls the covers down so they're just above his boxers. I can't help but stare. I think I'm going to drool in a minute; it's like the path to the Holy Grail or something.

I look back up and see the glint of mischief in his eyes. I put my coffee down on the table, take a deep breath, and lean over and kiss him. While he is penetrating my lips with his tongue, I run my hands over his flat stomach. It's even better in reality. He groans and says into my mouth, "God, Snow. Touch me again, please!"

I smile and kiss him harder.

I can feel all the contours of his six pack and I need to look at him, so I pull away from his mouth and straddle his chest. I slowly push myself down his body and kiss him on his chest, along to his nipple. I take it in my mouth and flick my tongue over it. I look up at him and he's watching me intently. I smile and then nip at his nipple.

"Ow … Snow!" he warns me. "You are treading on dangerous ground doing that."

"You love it really."

"Yes, I sure do." He leans his head back as I move my way over to the other nipple. I flick it, lick it, and nip it. He groans through it all. I slide further down his body and kiss each of the contours on his six-pack.

"Do you like that, Spence?" I ask, as he

groans again. I can feel how much he likes it; his cock is pressing against my stomach. It feels huge.

He doesn't give me any warning, but somehow I end up underneath him. He has me pinned to the bed now. I start laughing. "How ... how did you do that?"

"Where there's a will, there's a way. I need you underneath me, now." He lifts the t-shirt he had given me to wear last night and he moans when he sees my tits. "God, you're even more beautiful than I thought. I want to see if you taste as good as I think you do."

He doesn't wait for me to answer him, he just bends his head and copies what I did to his nipples. It feels really good. I can't believe I have gone five years without someone tasting my nipples. I arch my back. "Spence!"

He stops. "Yeah?"

"Don't stop, please. I need you. I want you so bad."

He chuckles. "The feeling is mutual, babe." He gets back to tasting my nipples, and then his hand goes lower. I gulp. This is it ... there's no going back after this. I don't know what to expect. What if I'm shit in bed? What if I don't know how to do what he wants to do? What if he's into kinky stuff? That scares me.

"Spence?"

He stops what he's doing and looks up to me. "Yeah?" He sticks his tongue out and runs it around my belly button while he's looking at me.

"You're not into kinky shit, are you?"

He laughs so hard. "No, babe. I'm not vanilla, but I'm not into kinky shit!"

I put my head back down. "Thank fuck for that. Carry on!"

He bends his head and moves that little bit further down my body. I gulp and hold my breath. My mind is going mad with my thoughts. I hope he kisses me between my legs … I'm so embarrassed he's going down there … I want him to be there … Oh my God. What do I want?

He doesn't give me a choice, he makes the decision for me. He looks up at me, slowly kisses my lips, and then sticks his tongue out and licks my clit. I throw my head back and press it into the pillow. "Oh my God. Oh my God!"

He chuckles and it vibrates through me. It turns me on even more. He takes his finger, runs it along the inside of my lips, and slowly pushes one finger inside me. It feels amazing. I haven't been intimate with anyone since Ethan and I'm going through a multitude of emotions. He takes his finger out and puts two in. I'm climbing the walls. I stretch out my arms and push his face closer to me. I need more.

Just when I think he's going to remove his fingers, I get the tightness from my toes and through my body, and I start bucking my body and screaming out his name. "Oh my God, Spence! Stop … Don't stop … Oh God, I don't know anymore."

He laughs and carefully removes his fingers and takes the last lick of my clit. He then crawls up my body and kisses me. I can taste myself on him. It tastes sweet and warm.

"I think you liked that, Snow." He chuckles.

"Hell yeah. I want more though. I want you inside me now, Spence."

"What's a man to do? Do I obey you or do I make you some breakfast?" He laughs as he leans over to his bedside table. He takes out a condom and rips open the packet, rolling it over his cock, and I can't help but stare. It's huge. He is never going to fit that inside me … never!

"I think I'll obey you. Do you want that? Do you want me inside you now?"

I nod my head frantically. "Yes, yes, yes."

I reach out, grab his arse, and start pushing him in. He doesn't let me take control, he looks at me as if to say *no*. So I let go and let him lead the way.

He pushes an inch inside and it feels amazing. My eyes open wide and he smiles at me. "More?" he asks.

I nod and he pushes another inch inside. I keep nodding my head, and painfully slowly, he pushes inch by inch until he is fully inside. I have tears in my eyes. I don't know why, but the way he went so slowly just triggered something in me. He cares.

"Are you okay? I didn't hurt you, did I?" he asks, as he starts to pull out.

I quickly put my hands on his arse and push him back in. "You are not going anywhere. I'm just emotional, but you haven't hurt me at all. Just give me a minute and then please fuck me!"

He chuckles and it sends me over the top.

"Actually, don't wait. Just fuck me now!"

He does, and it is amazing - out of this world. When he collapses on top of me, he kisses me gently and says, "That was better than I ever imagined. You drive me crazy, Snow."

He rolls off me, goes into the bathroom to

clean himself up, and then comes back to the bed. This is when it could get awkward. It doesn't. He sits up against the pillow and pulls me into his side. He kisses me on the head. "I really like you. I want this to work, I really do."

"I really like you too," I mumble into his chest.

We spend the next hour just talking about our lives and how we ended up here. He knows about Ethan but he didn't know how we ended up on our own and how Ethan has no part in our life. He was shocked when I told him how Ethan left me that night when I was still unconscious and never looked back. He never came back to me. Didn't want to know how I was, whether I had a child or not. As soon as I was well enough, Mum and Dad collected me and I left the States and came home.

I finally make a move to get home and he drops me off outside. I kiss him and he hugs me. "When can I see you again, Snow?"

"I'll see what I can arrange. I know I'll miss you."

"Me too, babe." He kisses me one last time and then I walk into the house.

"I'm home!" I shout, and I nearly get run over by Gracie.

"Mummy, where were you? I was so worried." She has her arms around my neck and is kissing me.

I let her down to the ground.

"Mummy went out with her friend. I had a good time. But I missed you so much."

"Did you have a sleepover? I want a sleepover with my friend too," she says matter-of-factly, with her hands on her hips.

"We can arrange for you to have a sleepover too. Whose house do you want to go to for a sleepover?" I ask her.

She slowly lowers her hands from her hips, "I'm not sure. I want to think about it. I'll let you know when I know."

I laugh; she looks so bossy, but then her vulnerability comes out.

"I love you, Mummy," she says, kissing me on the cheek.

"I love you too, Gracie."

WHISKEY SOUR

SNOW

Spence and I see a lot of each other over the next couple of months. Well, as much as I can as a single mother. My parents are really good and they help all the time. Mum knows I need to have some time for just me, and she regularly takes Gracie overnight for me so I can go out, have fun, and stay with Spence.

I stayed over last night, and while we're lounging in the bed, he leans over to kiss me. His kisses feel so amazing; he sets my world on fire. "God, Spence. I love when you kiss me." I groan into his mouth.

"Right back at ya, babe." He kisses me harder and forces his tongue inside. He pulls away after a few minutes.

"What's wrong?" I ask, running my hands over his chest.

"I have to go to work."

"What? You don't usually work during the day." Is he pushing me away?

"I know. Sawyer is in today with the accountants and they're doing a full stock check. It only happens once a year and I have to be there as the bar is my baby." He smiles. He loves his job, and sometimes it gets in the way of our relationship because he can't go out much, but we have so much fun at the club that I don't mind meeting him there. The fun always starts when we're alone together anyway.

"Sucks to be you," I say, laughing.

"Why don't you come over later, say lunchtime? Sawyer and Whiskey always get lunch in for us as we need to work through and be ready for opening hours. What do you think?"

He kisses me once more, but this time it's soft and gentle, and I can feel all his emotions pouring into my mouth.

"I'd love that. I'll go home now and get

Gracie settled at pre-school and then I'll swing by and meet you." I start to get out of bed, but he has other ideas and pulls me back down and devours my mouth.

I laugh.

"That's better," he says. "Now I can taste you all morning while I work." He gets out of the bed and heads towards the shower. I don't follow him like I want to. We would be there for another hour and we both need to get out on time this morning.

After we are dressed and in the car park, we kiss once more and then we go our separate ways.

When I get home, Gracie is up and looking out of the window for me. She smiles when she sees me and my heart skips a beat. I love her unconditionally and I thank my lucky stars for the day she came into my life. Thinking of her always makes me think of Ethan. I get angry now. I was devastated for the first couple of years and then I slowly became grateful for my relationship with him as it gave me Gracie. My anger is always directed at him. He deserted me at a time when I needed him the most. I never heard from him again; he obviously didn't love me as much as I loved him. That saddens me, because I thought he was my one, my only, my everything.

When I open the front door, Gracie throws herself at me. "Mummy, you're home. I missed you!" She kisses me all over and I laugh.

"I missed you too, baby. Right, let's go and get some breakfast and you can tell me all about your night."

Mum is already in the kitchen when I walk in with Gracie wrapped around my neck. "Morning, Mum. Was she good last night?" I ask, kissing Gracie all over her face.

Mum laughs. "She's always good, you know that. Do you want some bacon?"

"I'd love some," I say, bending down to put Gracie in her chair. She holds on until the last minute and then lets go and her body flops into the chair. I laugh. "You little monkey."

We eat our breakfast, and Mum and I chat about the plans for the day. "Gracie has dancing this morning. I'll take her. Can you pick her up, though? I'm going to Whiskey Sour to meet Spence for lunch. He has some stocktaking thing on or something."

"Of course. You won't be staying out again tonight, will you?"

"No. You know I only do it once a week." I smile at her. She and Dad have made my life so much easier by being here for me and helping with Gracie.

"I know." She laughs. "I just thought a beautiful woman like you would have more ..." She coughs. "Erm ... *needs* than once a week." She blushes but her redness will never match the colour of my face.

"MUM!" I splutter, and she laughs. "I can't believe you said that." I join in the laughter.

"I remember what it was like being young and in love, you know, Snow?" She is still laughing.

I put a finger in each ear, close my eyes, and shake my head. "La, la, la, la," I keep saying, ignoring her talk about her and Dad. I don't need to be thinking about that.

When I stop chanting and open my eyes, Mum has tears of laughter running down her face. Gracie is laughing and she has her fingers in her ears too.

I laugh. "Mum, stop! I don't need to have those visuals."

This is what I love. The easy camaraderie that we share, and this is what I want for Gracie. With my parents' help, we're passing this on to her.

When we've all calmed down, I help Mum with the dishes and she agrees to collect Gracie from dancing.

It always brings a tear to my eye when Gracie has her dancing clothes on. She reminds me of when I was young. She reminds me of my dancing abilities and how I'm not dancing anymore. I miss it, sometimes more than I know.

"Come on, baby. Let's go and show Rachel how you can do a pas de chat." She smiles and starts skipping down the corridor to the front door.

"Bye, Mum. See you later. I won't be late home, I promise."

"See you later, Snow. Have fun." Then she starts laughing. God, she is making me blush again.

We pull up outside Pointed Toes Studio and run across the car park and inside. Rachel opens the door and Gracie kisses her.

"Morning, Gracie," she says, and then looks up to me. "Morning, Snow. How are you today?" She hugs me.

Rachel was in my classes when I was a student at Sadler's Wells. We have been friends since we were very small.

"I'm good, thanks. Before I forget, Mum is

collecting Gracie today. I'm going to meet Spence for some lunch." I smile.

"I can't wait to meet this guy who puts that smile on your face. It's been a long time since we saw it."

"Thanks, and yes, he does put a huge smile on my face."

She leans closer and asks, "I know you don't like to dance, but can you just do a few steps? Gracie has been telling the others about you and they are dying to see for themselves."

I roll my eyes. I don't like to dance. Full stop. It brings back too many emotions and I don't feel ready, but if it's something Gracie wants me to do then, of course, I will do it. I nod.

"Good. I have my shoes in my office. I'll go and get them for you. I think we're still the same size." She scurries off to find her shoes.

Gracie walks over to me. "Mummy, are you going to dance for us?"

I nod my head and smile. "Yes, I am, baby. Do you want me to dance?"

She nods her head enthusiastically. "Yes, Mummy. I want to show my friends how good you are." She runs back over to her friends and they all start jumping up and down.

Rachel comes back and hands me the shoes.

I sit down on one of those small school benches. With my height, my knees nearly hit my eyes when I sit. I take my time putting on her ballet shoes and remember the whole routine all over again.

My feet feel uncomfortable in them, not like they used to feel. My feet must have changed shape now that they're not bound in my ballet shoes all the time. I squeeze them a little to make them more supple and then I stand and walk into the centre of the room.

Rachel claps her hands and all the dancers run into a line next to each other and fall silent. Wow, that is powerful.

"Today, we have a little surprise for you. Gracie's mum, Snow, is going to dance for you. She used to travel around the world ballet dancing every night. Are you ready?"

They all jump up and down and clap their hands. Once again, Rachel claps her hands and they fall silent, but with smiles on their faces.

My heart is pumping. I'm so nervous, but excited at the same time. I start dancing to a tune in my head. The Dance of the Sugarplum Fairy – this has always been my favourite dance.

I point my feet to each beat. It's feels like all the years have fallen away and I'm on that stage in New York. I can hear the music in my head, every single beat, and as the song ramps up in speed, I do a pas de chat and flick my feet up to my knees. It's so dainty and fluid. I hear someone clap and know that it's Gracie; this is the move we practiced the other day.

When I do my pique turns in a full circle around the room, I hear Rachel take a deep breath. I love these, but it has been a while since I've done them. I don't get dizzy and I don't lose the momentum. When I finish, I give a bow, and everyone starts talking, clapping, and shouting at the same time. I flop to the floor in a heap.

"Mummy, are you okay?" Gracie says, running over to me. She falls down onto my lap and wraps her arms around me.

"Yes, I am," I say, even though tears are running down my cheeks. I hug her close and take comfort from her.

Rachel rushes over. "Snow, are you okay? Do you want a drink?"

"No, I'm fine," I say, removing Gracie and standing up again.

The other dancers run over. "You're amazing."

"You're beautiful."

"Gracie, your mum is fantastic."

I don't hear the rest of the girls, I just look at Gracie, and I can see how proud she is of me. It breaks my heart.

When Rachel gives me a drink, she says, "You shouldn't give up dancing. You are so graceful and beautiful. Fuck, Snow, you're wasted."

"Thank you so much. I can't dance like I used to. I've got Gracie now and she is my life." I feel like I'm going to burst out crying. What is wrong with me? I never think about dancing like this. I don't allow myself to think about it.

"Well, I think you're wasting an amazing talent. If you're not going to dance then you should teach other children to be as good as you are." Rachel reaches over and gives me a big hug.

I can hear Gracie's friends asking her when they can come over to our house to play. I laugh. Gracie looks so proud of me.

I take the ballet shoes off and rub my aching feet. Right now, I don't know how I managed to dance all the time if this is the pain I had in my feet. I know that, actually, the pain is a hundred times worse.

When I've composed myself and put my own shoes back on, I hand the pumps to

Rachel and then give Gracie a squeeze before leaving to go and see Spence.

SPENCER

When I woke up this morning and saw Snow lying in my bed, I realised I want her in my bed all the time. I know it won't happen yet and that I will have to wait, but I know what I want and I will make it happen.

As I let myself in the door at Whiskey Sour, Stig is waiting for me. He slaps me on the back.

"Hey, Spence! Didn't think you'd be able to drag yourself out of that lovely warm bed this early, especially not with your girl in there with you." He laughs his deep, throaty laugh.

"Fuck off, Stig," I say, trying to push him on the arm. Of course, he is built like a brick shithouse and doesn't even budge. This just makes him laugh louder and harder.

Jeannie walks through the door. "What are you laughing at?" she asks him, with her hands on her hips.

He looks at me. 'Erm, I was just talking to Spence about not being able to get out of bed, that's all!"

She looks at me and I say, "Yeah, right. He was telling me how he likes to be tied to the bed with you, Jeannie."

Back at ya, Stig man.

She gasps and her face drops into a smile. Her features relax and she says, "Baby, you know I'll do that to you anytime."

I laugh so hard and I can't look at him. I walk through the doors and I hear Jeannie telling him all the things she will do to him when she ties him up. I can't listen anymore. I know I'll be in trouble later on when he finds me.

Sawyer and Whiskey are sitting at the bar, drinking coffee, and their heads are close together. Whiskey smiles up at Sawyer and he gently reaches out his hand and runs it up the nape of her neck and slowly brings her towards him and kisses her softly on the lips. All the time they're kissing, they never break eye contact.

I clear my throat. "Jesus. I think I might need another shower this morning. It's hot in here!"

They don't stop kissing until they're ready, and then they turn to look at me.

Sawyer says, "You're timing isn't great this morning, Spence."

"Damn, Sawyer. You told me what time to be here."

Sawyer laughs and pushes another cup over to me and I sit down on the barstool next to his.

We go over the jobs we have to do today, and when we've finished our coffees, we all get to work.

Stig comes into the bar after a few hours and he has Snow with him. I look at her and smile. She really is beautiful and I'm falling so hard for her.

Of course, Stig looks mischievous when he says, "I know it's been a long time since you saw each other, but please try to keep it clean."

"Fuck off, Stig," I say, giving him the finger.

He chuckles and leaves the bar. Snow sits on the barstool and I pass her a coffee. "It's too early to drink," I say.

She laughs. "It sure is. So, where is everyone? It looks really different in here during the day. Wow!" She looks around as if it's her first time in here.

Just as we're looking around, Whiskey, Sawyer, Stig, Jeannie, and Tilda walk into the bar, and Stig is carrying the food with him. "Come on over and have some lunch," Whiskey says, smiling at us.

We sit around the stage and the food is placed on the table for us to help ourselves. They're a great team. Their friendship has stood the test of time and they have been through so much together that they will always be friends. I don't know the full story about Whiskey, but she and Jeannie had some really bad shit happen to them. Looking at them now, they look like they don't have a care in the world. I'm sure that's not true, but they hide it well.

"So, Snow, what do you do with your time these days?" Whiskey asks, as she munches on a sandwich.

"I have a four-year-old daughter who keeps me busy," she answers, looking at the floor.

I reach out my hand and touch her arm. "No one here is judgmental, Snow," I whisper. She smiles at me.

"Wow, yeah, that would occupy your time. Spence told me you were a ballet dancer before you had her. Is that right?"

She smiles and looks up at them all. "Yes. I danced with the New York Ballet and travelled a lot."

"Do you miss it? Dancing, I mean?" Jeannie asks.

Snow looks at me and her eyes glaze over. "Actually, I didn't think I did, but this morning, I dropped Gracie off for her ballet dancing class and they asked me to do a dance for them. I only practice at home with her and I didn't really want to do it, but she looked at me with those puppy dog eyes and I danced the Dance of the Sugarplum Fairy. It was an amazing feeling, but it hit me how much I missed it."

"Why don't you dance again if you miss it that much?" Whiskey asks.

"I couldn't leave Gracie," she says sadly. Then she looks at me and says, "I have too many things keeping me here."

I smile, and I think I even blush. She's talking about me. I take her hand, bring it up to my lips, and kiss it.

"You could dance close to home and not

travel. I'm sure there are places you could dance in London theatres."

"I know, Whiskey, but I'm not sure I could do it all the time. It's so intense and the diets are strict, and I can't do anything else when I ballet dance. There would be no room in my life for anything else … or anyone else." She looks at me and squeezes my hand.

"You never know. Now that you've danced again, it might be something you want to pursue. If you do, let us know. We would love to see you dance."

"Thank you so much," Snow says, with a huge smile on her face.

We all laugh and joke for the next half an hour and then Sawyer claps his hands. "Right, back to work everyone. Let's get this stock take done and we can all go home for a couple of hours before the madness begins again."

Tilda takes the plates and leftovers out to the kitchens, Stig and Jeannie go back out to the office to look at the membership and accounts, and Whiskey and Sawyer go to his office to look over the accounts and do a general stock take. Well, that's what they say they're doing, but knowing the two of them, they will be up to no good. I have regularly caught them in the middle of some kind of foreplay or other. I'm used to it now; I just turn around and walk out of the room.

It's just Snow and me, and she sits on the barstool while I get back to my work. "I have to go down to the basement to check on some of the barrels. Will you be alright up here on your own for a bit?"

She laughs. "Of course I will. I'm not five, you know?"

I walk around to her side of the bar, open her legs, and walk in between them. I tip her chin up with my finger. "I know that, but I don't want you to be bored." I lean down gently and kiss her on her juicy, full lips.

She smiles. "I won't. Go do what you have to do, and the quicker it's done, the quicker you can take me home and fuck me." She looks me right in the eye.

My eyes open wide. "Holy shit, that really turns me on. Talk to me like that again." I kiss her and then whisper in her ear when I pull away. "Tell me you want me to fuck you."

She looks me directly in my eyes and says, "Spence, I want you to take me back to your place and fuck me … hard."

I growl, take her lips, and devour her again. God, she turns me on.

She gently pushes me away from her. "Go

work!"

I laugh and get back to my job, leaving her a few minutes later to go down to the basement.

SNOW

I want Spence so bad. My feelings for him are so intense that I know I want to take our relationship to the next level. I want him to meet Gracie. This is huge for me. I hope he wants to meet her too. We can talk about it later, after he has fucked me. I giggle.

Spence has been gone for about ten minutes when I decide to have a wander around the club. It's bright, and I walk towards the stage and run my fingers along it. I jump up onto it so I'm sitting on it and I look out at the tables. I can imagine it full of people watching the dancers on stage. I feel the pull to be on the stage. I stand up and spin around. God, the feeling of dancing on the stage and everyone being mesmerised by what they see is unbelievable. I really miss it.

I can hear music, and it's a classical song. As I walk around the stage just feeling the atmosphere in here, I start to move my body. I love classical music because it suits ballet the most. Before I know what's happening to me, I'm lost in thought and lost in the music.

I do pas de chats, pique turns, plies, spins, and so much more. I feel alive! I'm totally lost in the moment and one song moves into another and another. This is where I belong … on the stage, but I know I don't want to give my new life up either.

WHISKEY

Sawyer has two fingers inside me, teasing me, sucking my clit further into his mouth. "God, Sawyer. I need to come."

He moves his mouth away from my body. "I'm not stopping you, babe. That's my objective." He chuckles, and when he does that around my clit, he hooks his finger and I come all over them.

I throw my head back. "I love you so much, Sawyer."

He slows down his fingers and moves himself up my body and kisses me. I can taste myself on him and I love it. He finally removes his fingers and sucks them. He puts them in my mouth and makes me lick them clean. God, I love that.

I reach down to his hard cock and undo his belt and zip. His eyes open wide in anticipation. Just as I reach my hand inside, the office phone rings. I smile and ignore it. It keeps ringing and ringing.

"I'll answer it," Sawyer says, and I pull his trousers and boxers down. His cock springs up in front of me. I smile and lick my lips.

He looks at his cock and then at my face and says, "WHAT DO YOU WANT?"

I giggle and lick the tip, my eyes never leaving his.

"Spence, if this isn't important I will fucking kill you."

He points down to his cock, silently telling me to go on. I slide it in my mouth, with my lips strained over my teeth. He listens intently to Spence, "Mmmm, yeah ... you really want to talk to her NOW?"

I giggle as I pull it out of my mouth. Sawyer looks pissed. He hands the phone to me. "It's for you! You're going to finish that after that call, right?"

I nod and giggle. After taking the phone, I wipe my mouth with the back of my spare hand and wink at Sawyer. I sit on the desk and look at him sitting in his big chair.

"What do you want, Spence?" I ask.

"You need to look at the cameras in the bar, now!"

"Why? What's going on?" I'm instantly on alert. I always get worried that something bad is going to happen to us after everything that went down with Bomber and Stevo.

"Nothing bad, just something you need to see." I'm slightly distracted by Sawyer, who has his hand wrapped around his cock and is slowly pumping it up and down.

"Sawyer, sorry to disturb you there." I giggle. "Turn the cameras on in the bar. Spence says there's something I need to see."

He groans and goes to put his cock away, but I shake my head. He chuckles and leans over to turn the cameras back on.

I look at all the cameras, but there are two that have my instant attention. They face the stage, and Snow is dancing.

"Do you see it?" Spence says in a whisper.

"I'll ring you back," I say, and hang up.

I watch her dancing across the stage; she is absolutely mesmerising. It feels like I'm in a trance watching her. "Sawyer." I thump his arm without actually looking at him. "Do you see that? She is unbelievable!"

He leans forward; all thoughts of a blow job have disappeared. "Oh my God. Whiskey, you need to secure her to dance here. I don't know whether she would, but we need her. She will send the ratings right over the top. Fuck me, she is hypnotic!"

I lower myself down onto the chair and lean forward, resting my head in my hands as my elbows rest on the desk. We watch her spinning and pointing her feet and doing some weird step where it looks like she's kicking her own arse.

The music must be slowing down, because her movements are. I see the moment it stops because she collapses onto the floor. Spence runs onto the stage and pulls her towards him, and he hugs her and holds onto her. I can see her body bucking with sobs. I want to go to her and hold her, but instead, I turn and look at Sawyer. "She's a broken soul. I need her here. She would be so good for us, and we would be so good for her."

"Babe, you do whatever it takes to get her. She will take you places you never knew you wanted to go." He leans forward and kisses me, and his cock starts to come to life again.

I shake my head. "Sorry, not this time,

Sawyer. I have to go and speak to Snow before she leaves." I lean in and kiss him again. "I love you, and we can resume this," I say, pointing between us, "in a short while. Don't leave and don't do your trousers up!"

He chuckles and nods. He might be in charge, but sometimes, just sometimes, he lets me boss him about.

SNOW

I collapse in a heap on the stage the minute the music stops. Spence shouts, "Snow!" I hear him running towards me. "Babe, come here." He gathers me up and sits me on his lap on the stage. "You were amazing. Come on. Stop crying."

"I miss it so much, Spence, I really do," I say between sobs. "I didn't realise I missed it. I've managed to go through the last six years not thinking about it because I've had Gracie to think about. Today has made me realise I do miss it, but I know I can't go back to it."

He kisses me on the top of my head and rubs my back at the same time. "It's okay to grieve for something you can't do anymore. You are so talented. It's such a shame to waste your talent by not dancing anymore."

"I know, but I can't. Not with Gracie."

He holds me tight. "There has to be some way around it. I'll help you with whatever you want to do. I know this isn't the right time to tell you this, Snow, but I love you. I have fallen so hard for you. I want my forever with you, and I want to give you whatever I can to make you happy." He lifts my face up and kisses me softly at first, but increasing the pressure.

He loves me! Wow, I can't believe he told me he loves me. That makes me want to cry even more.

When he pulls away, he rests his forehead on mine.

"I love you too, Spence. It's getting harder to spend time away from you. I feel like I'm missing a part of me when I'm not with you."

He smiles at me. "Do you think you'd let me erm … erm … meet Gracie soon? I'd really like to meet her."

I know he has to meet her, but I'm worried. What if we don't work out and she's met him? What if she doesn't like him? What if he doesn't like her?

"Snow, stop it! Stop thinking about all the negatives all the time. It will be fine." He kisses me again.

"Excuse me."

We pull apart and turn to look at Whiskey, who is standing in front of the stage with her arms folded and a smile on her face.

"I'm sorry, Whiskey. I didn't mean to distract him from his work," I say hastily, trying to stand up and let Spence go back to work. He stands next to me and takes my hand.

"Come here, both of you," she says. We oblige.

"Snow, take a seat. Spence, go rustle up a couple of drinks for us, please."

He smiles and makes his way to the bar.

I take a seat and look at her. I'm about to start apologising again when she holds her hand up in front of my face.

"Snow, let me talk, please. I have something I want to say to you."

"Okay," I mumble. She's scaring me.

"I know you've been through something terrible in your life. I can see it in your eyes. Jeannie and I went through something horrific a few years ago and we found solace here in Whiskey Sour. We met some wonderful people who helped us to make this place fantastic and we buried some ghosts along the way."

Spence comes over and hands us a cocktail

each. "A Whiskey Sour for you both." He leans down and kisses me before walking back to the bar.

"I watched you dancing just now, and I have to tell you that I have *never* seen anyone dance like that before in my life. Believe you me, I have watched a lot of dancers over the years, and no one has intrigued me or enthralled me as much as you just did. I was making out with Sawyer in the office and I left him with his cock out because I wanted to come out here and talk to you."

I blush. She did not just say that, did she?

She laughs. "Don't worry," she says, looking at my stunned expression. "He'll still be there when I get back. He won't miss out."

I am stunned! "O ... kay! Thanks?"

She laughs again and takes a sip of her drink. When it slides down her throat, she closes her eyes, and it's like she's really savouring every drop. She opens her eyes and looks at me.

"Snow, would you consider coming to dance for me here at Whiskey Sour? I know it's not the kind of dancing you're used to, but when I saw you on that stage, I just knew that you are destined to dance again. I think we could work together really well. What do you think?"

"Wow, I'm not sure." I don't know what to say. She's offering me the opportunity to dance, but she expects me to take my clothes off. I don't know how I feel about that.

"What are you not sure about, Snow? Is it the stripping part of it?" I nod my head. "You know, we're not strippers. We're dancers foremost. Some of the girls never take their clothes off. They tease the audience with a dip of the shoulder here and a look over the shoulder there. Burlesque is all about tease. It's not crass. It's sensual and sensitive."

I take a sip of my drink; my mind is racing.

Whiskey goes on. "Look, I know you've seen the show and you know it's not tacky. What you probably don't know is that the girls have dance sessions with Beau three times a week. This keeps them in shape and keeps the dances new. Why don't you come along to the next session, join in, and see what you think?"

"I've only ever danced ballet though. I wouldn't be able to dance to pop music."

She laughs. "We can play classical music here as well, you know? Why don't you just come along and talk to Beau? He will help you. I promise you will love it. Beau works very closely with Nate, our music guy, to create the best music for the girls."

"Can I think about it? I want to talk to Spence about it before I make a decision. Thank you for believing in me. I really appreciate it."

"Of course you can think about it. I would never push anyone to work here. I think you would fit in really well with the other girls and I know everyone would want to see you dance." We sit in silence for a while and finish our drinks.

Spence comes over and sits with us. "So ... am I forgiven for interrupting your, erm ... meeting?" He laughs.

"Shit! I forgot he was still in there waiting for me. Gotta run! Talk to you soon, Snow, and think about what I said." She stands up, waves into the air, and runs out of the room.

"What was she doing?" I ask Spence. He's laughing.

"She was waving to Sawyer to let him know that she's on her way back to him. See, there are cameras everywhere." He points them out to me; I hadn't noticed them before.

"Is that how she knew I was dancing?"

"Kind of. I saw you when I came back from the basement and I rang her and told her to look at the cameras. I didn't want her to miss out on seeing you up on that stage. Sorry if I did the wrong thing."

I lean over and kiss him. "No. You didn't do the wrong thing. You might just have given me the hope I need to go forward in my life. She offered me a job, but I'm guessing you knew she would when you told her to watch me dance."

He blushes. "I hadn't seen you dance, but I will hold my hands up and say that I have Googled you. Don't hate me."

I laugh. "I can't believe you did that."

"Yeah, I did. But nothing compares to what I witnessed today. You should do this, you know? Not just because I get to see more of you, but because you need to do it for yourself."

"I need to have a think about it because I'm not sure I can do the whole burlesque thing. Whiskey told me to come in for the next session that the girls will be having with Beau and see what he thinks and whether he could help me with some more appropriate music."

"That is a great idea, but God, he is *so* annoying."

I laugh as he tells me story after story about Beau. We've moved back over to the bar so he can finish his stock take.

"Right, that's the last bit done now. I'm going to take this to the office, and when I get back, we can be on our way." He kisses me again. I love his kisses.

He's back within five minutes, smiling. "They'd finished whatever 'meeting' they had." He shakes his head. "Come on, babe. Let's get out of here."

He takes my hand and leads me out of the bar. We walk past the office where Stig is still looking over the books with Jeannie. As we wave and say goodbye, Jeannie pops her head out.

"Snow. It would be great to have you on board with us. I saw you dancing earlier; you were amazing." She smiles and then ducks back into the office.

I look at Spence. "Did you ring her too?"

"I was looking for Whiskey and I spoke to Stig. I guess they must have turned their cameras on the stage too. Sorry, not sorry!" he says, holding his hands up in the air and shrugging his shoulders. He grabs my hand again and we walk out to his car.

Thirteen

2 WEEKS LATER

SNOW

Spence dropped me home straight after his stock take because it had taken longer than expected. He told me he loved me again when we said goodbye.

I am so excited and nervous about today. Two very important things are happening. The first is that I'm going in to Whiskey Sour for a dance rehearsal with Beau. I'm sweating just thinking about it. My style of dance is so different to theirs and I just can't see how we're going to be suited. Secondly, Spencer is coming over for tea and he is going to meet

Gracie for the first time. I'm dreading it. I've told her that Mummy has a boyfriend and his name is Spence, so she has heard me talking about him and she's looking forward to meeting him.

After dropping her at her ballet class, I wave to Rachel and then make my way over to Whiskey Sour. I'm really nervous about meeting Beau. Spence says I'll like him, but it doesn't stop me shaking when I'm in the car park. I take a deep breath and decide that I have to pull my big girl pants up, and I walk to the front door.

After knocking, Stig opens the door and smiles at me with a wide grin. "Come on into the mad house, Snow."

I smile. "Thanks, Stig. I'll see you later."

"You sure will." He smiles.

When I reach the door to the bar, I grab it, take a deep breath, and swing it open with a confidence I'm not feeling.

Beau – well, I believe it's Beau - sees me and runs over.

"Oh my God! I can't believe you're here and are going to be dancing with me. I love you!"

I laugh, and all of a sudden, my tension has fallen away. He pulls me into a hug and guides me towards the other girls. I've met them before when I've been waiting for Spence to finish up.

"Hey, girls. You know Snow already. Let's huddle!" Beau says, clapping his hands.

The girls come over to us and give me a big group hug. This is weird!

When we pull apart, the girls start talking at once. Beau says, "Now, girls. Give Snow some space." They all stop talking. "We're going to do a warm up and then we would really like to see you dance," he says nervously.

"Yeah, no problem. I'm nervous though, just so you know."

"We were all nervous when we first did this," Dee Dee says. "Why don't we all do a little number first, just to help your nerves?" She smiles at me and the other girls agree.

Beau puts on some music and they do a dance. They are really good, and Baby is so cute she's funny. Sissy is so sexy, she makes me blush, and when Jeannie did her dance, it was all old-fashioned carnival type dancing.

I clap after they've finished. "Wow, girls. Now I feel even more inadequate." Then I laugh. "Beau, do you have anything classical for me to dance to? That's all I've ever danced to."

I feel stupid now. How did I think this was

going to work? They all dance to modern music, not classical.

"I am prepared," he says, fiddling with his CD player. "Go get ready on the stage and then I'll put something on for you. Just go with the music and show us what you've got!" He smiles to make me feel at ease.

I get up on the stage, stand in the middle, and wait. Everything is silent. Then I hear it … a beat, then another beat. It is something classical, but not something I've heard before. I dance to the tune. I spin, I pas de chat, plie, and jump. Before I know what's happening, the song is finished and all the girls start clapping. Beau has tears in his eyes when he jumps up on the stage to hug me. "I have never seen ballet danced like that before, Snow. You are so graceful and beautiful."

"Thank you." I blush.

"Come on. Let's get a drink and see what we can do with your style." He takes my hand and we jump off the stage together.

The girls all run and hug me. "Well done, Snow. That was amazing," Jeannie says. The rest of them agree with her.

Beau claps his hands. "Right, girls. Now we need to work out a routine for Snow, and what about changing the finale so that we can incorporate the right kind of music for her to dance to? How do you feel about that?"

The girls agree. "We like new routines," Jeannie says, smiling.

"Snow, you will soon be able to put your signature moves into any type of music. Wait until you get a chance to do the freestyle! That will test your skills."

"Ooh, I love freestyle," Baby says sweetly.

"Yeah, me too," says Wanda.

"I can't wait to give it a go," I say, but really I'm dreading it. I haven't danced ballet to anything other than classical music. I don't think this is going to work. I take a drink and sit down for a few minutes while Beau works with the other girls.

After another hour, we take a break, and Beau comes up to me and puts his arm around me. "So, what do you think, Snow? Do you think you could do this?"

"To be honest, Beau, I really don't know. I'm not used to dancing ballet to pop music and that scares me."

"I know it does. You are such a great dancer so you should be able to dance to any music. You can take a piece of music and envisage moves around the stage to it. I can then help you to make it more 'burlesque', more sexy.

What do you think? Do you want to give it a go?"

I think about what he says, and yes, if I am a good dancer then I should be able to dance to any music. I've been to enough auditions in my time where I have had to make up a dance on the spot, but that was different. It was always classical music.

"Beau, I really want to do this. The girls are fantastic and they have made me so welcome. I've come to realise that I really, really want to dance again. But I'm scared. I don't know if I can do it."

"Snow, you were a prima ballerina. You danced in amazing theatres around the world – you can do whatever you put your mind to!"

"Thanks, Beau. If you help me then I'd love to give it a go."

"That is great news. Okay, I have a song that I think is just perfect for you. It's classical, operatic, and then it breaks into pop music and then back to classical. I've trimmed it so it fits into our timescale and isn't too much classical at the beginning. Do you want to hear it?"

"Yeah, I would love to," I say, with a smile on my face. "I'm really excited."

Beau goes to his sound system and turns the music up. "Snow, this is music from the Bruce

Willis film *The Fifth Element*."

The music that comes out is haunting and operatic, just like he said. I find myself thinking of moves I could make to this music. As my mind drifts off into a different place, the music changes to a pop sound. It's fast paced and has a real beat to it. Just as I'm getting the tune in my head, it changes to a mixture of both. There's the beat and then the operatic singer is back. I absolutely love it. I have a grin across my face.

"Well?" Beau asks, with a hint of trepidation.

"I love it, Beau. Thank you." I hug him. He claps his hands and we all laugh at him.

"Now we just have to put some moves to it. I'll give you a copy of this and you can listen to it overnight, and then tomorrow, when we do a class, we can see what you have and I can make a few suggestions. We can go from there."

"Fantastic. Thank you so much for believing in me."

"Girl, with the way you dance, it would be hard not to believe in you!" He has the biggest smile I have ever seen on his face.

We pick up our things and make our way out to the front door. I see Stig there and I say hi. Spence isn't in yet so I decide to go and surprise him before he has to go to work. I'm high after the dance session and I can't wait to tell him all about it.

I ring my mum to let her know that I won't be home for another hour or so.

When I get to Spence's apartment, I knock on the door, and it's only when I'm standing there that I think maybe I should have rung. What if he's busy or has someone here? I start to panic.

I needn't have worried. When he opens the door, he has the biggest smile on his face. He looks shocked to see me but I can see he likes my surprise. I follow him inside.

"This is a nice surprise. What did I do to warrant a visit from you?" he asks, pulling me in close for a kiss.

He makes me melt when he kisses me. "I just missed you, that's all," I say, kissing him back.

"Mmm, that's allowed."

When I step back, I realise he must have just got out of the shower, because he's shirtless and his lower half is covered by a small towel wrapped around his waist. I can feel his cock coming to life.

I mould myself into him more so I can feel

him rubbing against me.

"I was just getting ready for our dinner date with Gracie," he says, walking to his bedroom and pulling me by my hand. "Now I've changed my mind. Now I just want you."

When we get to his bedroom, he kisses me hard. While he's kissing me, I undo his towel. It slides to the floor and he smiles in my mouth. I reach out and grab his already hardened cock. I love his cock; it fits me perfectly, like it was made especially for me.

"What are you doing, Snow?" he mumbles against my lips.

"I'm hungry after that hard workout at Whiskey Sour," I say, as I push him down onto the bed. His cock stands to attention and I slide down onto my knees.

"I like it when you're hungry." He groans as my fingers work their way up his legs to his balls. I take them in my hands as I kiss my way up his legs to his beautiful, hard cock.

I lick from the base to the tip, slowly … agonisingly slowly.

"Snow, please …" He groans, pushing his cock up into my face.

"In my own time, Spence … be patient. I promise it will be worth it."

"I know it will, just hurry up because I so

want to be in your hot, wet mouth." He thrusts his cock closer to my mouth.

I chuckle as his cock is resting between my lips. It jerks and I know he's desperate for me take him deep in my mouth. When I reach the tip of his cock, I lick the drop of pre-cum on the end. "Mmm," I say, flicking my tongue back and forth over the hole in the tip.

He's getting impatient, thrusting his body in my face. "Snow!"

I laugh and open my mouth, and very slowly take him in. I wrap one of my hands around the base and lower my mouth down until it touches my hand. The other hand is still wrapped around his balls, jiggling them. My lips tighten around his cock and I start fucking it with my mouth.

"Oh my God, Snow. I really love it when you're hungry."

I chuckle and he groans; he likes that. After working him with my mouth, I know I'm pushing him over the edge, and however much I like that, I want him inside me when he loses control.

I pull away and slowly crawl up his body, kissing him on the way. I reach his mouth and I devour it, I let him taste himself, let him see how good he tastes.

I pull away. "Spence, where ..." He doesn't give me a chance to say anything else, he just reaches out his hand and opens his drawer. He pulls out a condom and hands it to me. I smile and work my way back down to his cock.

I rip open the pack, put the condom in my mouth, and slowly work the condom over his cock. "Oh my God. Snow, that is fucking amazing."

I look up at him and smile when it's on. I move forward until my throbbing pussy is over the top of his cock. I reach behind me and grab it, and then I impale myself with it.

"God!" He groans.

I smile and sit still to get my breath back. He reaches up and takes my hands for me to brace myself on, and then I start to gyrate my hips, taking him as deep as I can. I lift myself up until I'm at the tip, and then I sit back down ... quickly.

We get into a rhythm, me pushing down as he pushes his cock up in time with my moves. I lean forward and he grabs me and kisses me. At the same time he has lifted his hips and he starts pounding my pussy.

I can feel the tension starting inside me; I know it won't be long. "Spence, I'm ... I'm going to come."

He pounds harder and deeper then my pussy starts pulsating on his cock and I lose control of myself. He follows immediately. He keeps pumping in and out but is slowing down, and then he hugs me to his body. "Wow. I definitely like it when you're hungry, Snow."

I laugh. "Yeah, me too." I climb off him and lay next to him with my hand rubbing his chest. "I love you, Spence. Thank you for pushing me to dance again."

"I love you too," he says, pulling me even closer to him. "I can't wait to hear how you got on today."

I spend the next ten minutes telling him about my day. Then he moves away from me. "Now, we need to move. I have a very important first date tonight and I need to get my A game on!" he says, pushing me out of the bed.

I laugh. "Yeah. I hear she is a tough cookie."

We get dressed and I drive us over to my house. Just before we get out of the car, Spence stops me by putting his hand on my leg.

"I'm nervous, Snow. What if she doesn't like me? I want you to be happy, and I know tonight is make or break for us, because if she doesn't like me then things are going to be awkward. Just remember I love you so much, and I don't intend to let you go that easily."

I turn to face him. "Spence, she will love you. Just be yourself and you'll be fine. I promise."

"Okay." He looks straight ahead. "Let's do this!" He turns and gets out of the car. I meet him in front of the car and he takes my hand and we walk towards the house.

When I open the front door, Gracie comes running up to me and jumps up to hug me.

"Mummy, Mummy! I'm so excited. I promise I'll be good." When I let her down, she realises Spence is with me. She walks over to him and holds her hand out for him to shake. "Hi, I'm Gracie. I'm very pleased to meet you."

I stifle a laugh; she has obviously been practicing all day.

He bends down and takes her hand. He pumps it up and down. "Hi Gracie. I'm Spencer, but you can call me Spence. I'm pleased to meet you too. Your mummy has told me so much about you. I heard that you are a good dancer, just like your mummy."

She smiles and lets go of his hand. "Yes, I am." She leans forward, cups her hand around her mouth, and whispers into his ear loud enough for me to hear, "Actually, I'm better!"

He laughs and she starts giggling. "Mummy, can I show him my bedroom?"

I nod. "Of course you can." I mouth to Spence that I'm sorry, but he just grins and shakes his head.

She takes his hand and starts telling him all about pre-school, dancing, and all her dolls, as she takes him upstairs to see her room.

I walk into the kitchen. "Can I help with anything, Mum?" I ask, looking around to see what I can do.

"No. Everything is ready. We just need to wait for madam to stop talking and bring Spence back downstairs to eat," Mum says, as she pours me a glass of wine.

We put everything on the table, and just as we're about to call them down, they walk into the dining room.

They're holding hands, and Gracie is saying, "So, that's a tour of the house. Do you have any questions?"

He looks at me and laughs. "Not right now, but if you sit next to me at dinner, then if I have any questions I can ask you. Is that okay?"

She smiles, sits down, and points at the chair next to her for Spence to sit. I think she likes him. Thank God for that. I didn't realise how important this moment really is.

Dinner is a success, and so is Spence. I think Gracie loves Spence as much as I do.

TWO MONTHS LATER

I stretch in bed and feel a hot, muscly body next to mine. Spence.

"Good morning, babe. Did you sleep well?"

"I always sleep well when I'm in your bed."

He laughs. "I hope that's because you know I'm here to protect you, but I think it might be because I wear you out the night before."

I blush and laugh because he is so right.

"So what are your plans today, Snow?"

"Well, after I ravish you," I say, running my finger down his hard torso. "I'm going home to take Gracie to dancing class and then I'm off to work."

"I'll meet you there later. I think I'm going to need some recovery time."

We have a shower together, but I think we need another one after all the things we did in there. When I'm dressed, I kiss him and drive home with a huge smile on my face.

Gracie is having breakfast when I get there, and I kiss her on the head.

"Mummy, when is Spence coming over? I miss him."

I feel bad because she wants to see him all the time and I don't want to annoy him. Sometimes I don't want to share him.

"Can he collect me from dancing before he goes to work? Please, Mummy?"

"I don't know, Gracie. I'll have to ask him."

"Yay! I know he will. He loves me." She smiles and skips off to get her ballet bag.

Mum laughs. "You've got competition there!"

"I know. I'll ring him now."

Of course, he agrees to pick her up. He's delighted she wants him to collect her.

She is so excited when I tell her. She runs out to the car and climbs in the front with the biggest grin on her face.

When we get to ballet, I speak to Rachel and tell her that Spence will collect her and take her home.

"No worries, Snow. Look at her. She's so excited, telling all her friends."

"She's been bouncing around the place all morning." I laugh. I kiss Gracie and tell her I'll see her later.

I smile when I get in the car. She is really growing.

Beau works us like troopers, and it's a couple of hours before we get a break. There is no one else in the club, the music has been turned up really loud, and we have been rocking it. He claps his hands and turns down the music.

"Now, girls. You can have a twenty minute break and then we start again. This new finale is going to be so special." He claps his hands again.

I take my drink and my small towel out of my bag, and use the towel to wipe my forehead. "God, I'm wrecked!"

"I know how you feel, hun," Sissy says, standing there with just her bra and knickers on. She has no shame, but then again, her body is amazing.

I take my phone out and see I have had ten missed calls from Mum, six missed calls from Spence, and loads of texts telling me to ring home immediately. Oh my God. What is going on? I hold my phone out and stare at it. I can feel my body start to shake.

"Are you okay, Snow? You've gone pale," Jeannie says, walking over to me. "Well, you know what I mean!" She touches my arm.

"Erm, I don't know. I think something's

wrong. I have to ring home."

I walk over to the bar and sit down. The house phone gets answered after the first two rings. *"Snow?"*

"Yeah. Dad, what's going on?"

"It's Gracie."

"Oh my God. What's happened?" I start to cry. Nothing can happen to my little baby. She is my life.

I hear a shuffle in the background and then I hear Spence. *"Babe, I'm coming to get you."* He's crying. This isn't good.

"Spence, tell me what the FUCK is going on!"

"Snow, she wasn't there when I went to collect her. Gracie wasn't there!"

"Were you late?" I shout, accusing him. My thoughts aren't straight right now.

"No, babe. I promise. Rachel said she was collected earlier by a guy and she thought it was me. She said that Gracie had gone out of the room to the toilet, and when she didn't come back in, a guy shouted through the door that he was supposed to pick her up today. I promise I was on time. I'm leaving now. I'll be with you in five minutes; the police will be here in ten!" He hangs up.

Jeannie walks around the other side of the bar and pours me a straight up whiskey. "Drink this. You look like you need it. It will make you feel better."

I down it in one and then slam the glass down. She takes it and pours me another, then another, then another. "Someone has Gracie. Jeannie, someone has my baby!"

By this time, all the girls are over, asking me questions and trying to hug me. I don't want their hugs, I want Gracie. I shrug them all off me.

"Get off me! I need to find her." I stand up and start pacing, walking around in circles. I don't really know what I'm doing.

Spence is true to his word. He walks in five minutes later. I run at him, and as he tries to pull me into his body, I don't want that. I start thumping his chest.

"I left you to collect her. Why did I do that? Why? You can't even pick her up and take her home."

As I'm shouting and hitting him, he stands there and takes it all. "Snow, please. We need to find her and then you can take it out on me. I AM going to find her, don't ever doubt that!"

I calm down and he gathers me into his body for a hug. I let him. I need the comfort he's offering me.

"Come on, babe. The police will be at your house soon. We will find her, I promise you we will, even if it's the last thing I ever do!"

Jeannie has got my bag for me, and she follows us out to Spence's car, which looks like he just abandoned it outside. She puts it on my lap as I sit in the passenger seat with tears running down my face.

"Spence, I'll ring Stig and Sawyer. They'll know what to do."

"Thanks, Jeannie."

Spence doesn't say anything all the way home. I think he is scared to say anything to me because he knows I blame him.

I run into the house as he has barely stopped the car.

"Mum! Mum!" I shout, and run into her arms. I finally let the tears fall again and she holds me up.

"Come on, baby. She'll be fine. No one would want to hurt her. She's probably just gone on an adventure and will come back in an hour or so." She rubs my hair like she used to when I was smaller.

I sniffle and she holds me tighter. The doorbell rings and we all look at the door. Spence goes to open it and there is a policeman and a policewoman on the other side.

"Hi. We're here about the missing girl. Can we come in, please?"

"Sure." He opens the door wide enough for them to come in. Dad leads them into the kitchen where we all sit around the table just looking at them.

"Have you found her yet?" I snap.

"No, sorry. We're here to get some more details so we can start looking for her."

"You mean you haven't even started looking for her yet?" I slam my hand down on the table.

"We need to get the basic information. Her name, age, a recent picture; that kind of thing. We need to know if there is someone who she would go with freely, and what is her understanding of strangers? Does she know not to talk to them and go anywhere with them?"

"She knows all of that! We have talked about 'stranger danger.' No one else would have collected her. Spence was supposed to collect her."

Spence puts his hand on my shoulder from behind me. I reach up and put my hand on top of his. I know it's not his fault that Gracie wasn't there for him to collect. I know it in my heart; it was just an automatic reaction.

We spend the next hour going through so many questions. What other male figure does she know? Who does she trust implicitly? Who knew she was at her ballet class? Who would want to take her and why?

We don't know the answers to the last couple of questions and I'm getting frustrated. This isn't helping to find her. All it's doing is wasting time.

"So many questions and you are still NOT out looking for her. Please just go and find her and then you can ask as many questions as you like. PLEASE!" I break down sobbing. I can't hold it in anymore. I feel sick and I run out to the toilet to vomit.

Spence comes in and holds my hair back for me. "She'll be fine. You know that, don't you? I promise I'll find her if it's the last thing I do. Stig, Sawyer, and Tilda's husband, David, are on their way. If someone needs finding, they are the ones to do it. I'll tell you Whiskey's story one day and you'll understand."

I lift my head out of the toilet and lean back into him. He kneels behind me and holds me while I sob uncontrollably.

SPENCER

As much as Snow is falling apart, I'm

finding it harder not to fall with her. I feel like it's my fault. Why didn't I get there earlier? Would it have made a difference? It was my first time being responsible for beautiful Gracie, and I fucked up. Where the fuck is she? Who has her? They better not hurt a hair on her head because I will seriously fuck with them if they do.

My life hasn't always been sugar sweet and niceties. I've had to graft my way up from the dirty streets. Whiskey seems to find lost souls and tries to help them; she certainly changed my life. I owe her and the lads my life, and I'll never forget it.

Snow is leaning against me, sobbing. I pick her up, carry her into the lounge, and lay her down on the couch. Her mum is being comforted by her husband.

The policeman says, "I think we've got everything we need. We will get on this straight away and start circulating her picture so we can get everyone on high alert. We'll ring you in a couple of hours to update you, if we've not already found her by then. Most of these cases are resolved when the child comes home after playing with their friends."

"She wouldn't go and play with anyone without telling us first," Snow's mum says, sniffling.

He walks to the door and I see him out.

As I walk into the lounge, my heart breaks for this family. Snow is barely conscious, her mum is shaking with the sobs, and her dad is as white as a sheet.

"I know Gracie is not my daughter, but she's worked her way into my heart. I will do EVERYTHING I can to bring her home. My friends who are coming around here in a few minutes can do this, but they will have to break the law. I'm just telling you so you know there will be no stone unturned or any streets not searched." I run my hands through my hair. I needed to tell them that the guys are not necessarily orthodox, but that they get the right results.

Snow's dad comes over to me and, uncharacteristically, he wraps his arms around me and hugs me. "Whatever you have to do to bring my Gracie home, you have my total backing, son," he whispers in my ear. I hug him back, and when we part, the front door rings. Snow shouts out, "Gracie!"

"Babe, it's the guys. Can we go into the kitchen to talk to them, please?" I ask her dad.

"Whatever it takes."

I go to open the door and the guys filter in

one at a time. Sawyer – the man who rescued Whiskey at a time when she needed him. Stig – tall, dark, and very fucking scary. He can be very intimidating and persuasive if he needs to be. David – I'm not sure what he does, but I think it's something in security, although I've heard some of the stories about him. His reputation precedes him.

"Straight ahead there, lads." I guide them past the lounge and into the kitchen. I've had personal dealings with the three of them and I'd much rather have them in my corner than as my enemy.

Snow's dad comes in and gets out a bottle of whiskey and some shot glasses, and places them on the table in front of us. "Take what you want and do whatever you have to to find my Gracie."

"Take a seat. We need you here. You have information that junior here doesn't," Sawyer says, nodding his head in my direction.

"Fuck off!"

Sawyer chuckles. "Spence, talk us through exactly what was supposed to happen and then what actually happened. Don't leave any details out because they could be vital," he says, pouring each of us a shot.

I tell them how Gracie wanted me to collect

her, how Snow agreed and even told Rachel, the dance teacher, I was coming to collect her. None of it was out of the ordinary except me collecting her instead of her granny.

"Do you think it could be your past catching up on you, Spence?" Stig asks.

David laughs. "There is absolutely no chance of that. None of your pasts will ever haunt you. I made sure of that. This has got to be something to do with Snow. This is where we need you to tell us anything you know about Snow and her past. Boyfriends, lovers, anything. No information is too much. We need to know everything."

Sawyer fills our glasses again and Snow's dad starts her story. He tells us about her life and moving to New York, then he talks about Ethan, Gracie's dad.

"Snow loved Ethan and thought she had met the man she was going to spend the rest of her life with." He looks up at me and mouths, 'Sorry'. I nod for him to continue.

"He loved her too, and to be honest, we thought everything was perfect. The night he proposed, she collapsed after the show and she had blood running down her legs." He stops and takes the shot Sawyer has poured for him.

"An ambulance came and took her to the ER

as she had passed out and they couldn't bring her round. While she lay in the hospital room, unconscious, he sat there looking like he was so worried, and held her hand. They asked him whether there was a chance she was pregnant and he said there wasn't. His demeanour changed after that. Later on, they brought in a sonographer, who performed a scan of her stomach as the pregnancy test had proved positive." He is really choked up; whatever happened next affected not only Snow, but her parents too.

"They thought she was having a miscarriage and needed to know if the baby was still alive. As soon as the scan was up on the screen, you could hear the beep, beep of Gracie's heartbeat, and the sonographer told him that the baby was still there, that she hadn't miscarried, and the baby seemed healthy." He takes another sip. Whatever is about to happen in Snow's story must be big, because he's filling up with tears.

"Erm ... sorry, but this is hard. Instead of him being elated that his new fiancée was pregnant and the baby was okay, he stood up and walked out of the hospital, never to be seen again. He abandoned her when she needed him the most. She was still unconscious, and when she came round, he wasn't there to comfort her or help her with the shock of being pregnant. Apparently, he had never wanted children. He wanted to travel the world dancing like they had for the previous few years. He was a selfish bastard, and if I ever get my hands on him, I have a few choice things to say to him."

I pace around the kitchen. I can feel my blood pressure rising, my cheeks getting redder. I want to punch something, which is something I haven't done in years. Actually, I want to kill someone, again, something I haven't done in years. How could someone do that to Snow? We never talked about Gracie's dad, but I'm sure she would have told me eventually, because I don't want her past to define whatever we have together. My heart breaks for her.

"Well, if I get my hands on him then it'll be my fists that do the talking."

"Calm down, Spence. This isn't going to help us find Gracie." Sawyer, ever the man of reason, says.

David clears his throat. "Do you think it could be Ethan?"

"I don't know. He didn't want anything to do with Snow or Gracie. I don't even know if he knows she kept her. He didn't come across as being capable of this, to be honest. We haven't heard from him since that day."

"I think we will look for clues as to who it was that took her, but I think we need to look at Ethan and see what his movements are too. Spence, I know it's not anyone from your past, and I don't think it's a totally random kidnap. So, we need to know everything we can about this Ethan guy and then we can see if we can track him down. What's his surname?" He leans down and takes his laptop out of his bag. I hadn't even seen him bring it in with him.

"Cross," Snow's dad says.

After placing it on the table, he logs into Google and starts to do his research on Ethan Cross. I leave them to do that while I go and check on Snow.

She's just lying on the couch, staring into space. I approach her and kneel down so I'm at the same height as her. "Hey, babe. The guys are here now. Everything is going to be alright. They WILL find her." I lean down and kiss her on the lips very gently. She doesn't need my passion. Right now, she needs my love and my comfort.

"Spence, I can't believe someone would take her. She is such a beautiful girl. So bubbly, and she's mine." She sobs again.

I take her hand and bring it to my lips to kiss. "Snow, we will find her. They're researching Ethan Cross at the moment."

Her eyes open wide when I say his name. "Ethan!" she says, rolling his name around her mouth like he's an old butt from a dirty ashtray. "You don't … you don't think he could have taken her?" She sits up. "Oh my God. It has to be him. The fucking bastard. When I get my hands on him, I'm going to fucking kill him. How dare he do this? All he had to do was ask to see her; I would have let him. Not now. He can go fuck himself on a fucking sword for all I care about him!"

My placid, beautiful girl is shouting and swearing and throwing her arms around the place. I smile; she has spunk and we need to build on that and use her energy to find him.

"Too right. That's if I don't find him first. Come with me into the kitchen and see the guys. You're the best person to be able to help them find her."

She takes my hand and stands up. We walk into the kitchen. This is not going to break us; it's going to make us stronger.

Fourteen

PAST CATCHES UP

SNOW

I have a knot in the bottom of my stomach and my heart is racing. Ethan fucking Cross! It has to be him; no one else would have any interest in my daughter. I don't have any money for someone to kidnap her for a ransom. Why would he do that? If he had asked me to meet her then I would have said yes. Even though he broke my heart and shattered it into a thousand pieces, he is her dad and he would have a right to see her. I wouldn't deny Gracie a chance to know her real dad. I wouldn't do that to her.

When I get into the kitchen, all the guys are huddled around David's laptop.

"Hey, guys. Thank you for coming to help me. I really appreciate it."

"Listen, Snow, you're one of us now. You're family. Whiskey Sour family. We protect our own. We need to ask you some questions to get a better handle on this Ethan guy," Sawyer says, pulling a chair out for me to sit down next to David.

"Listen, whatever it takes to get my daughter back. She will be so scared being with someone she doesn't know." I try not to think of what he might be doing to her. I need to concentrate on finding her. I will not break down! At least if Ethan has her then I don't think he would hurt her.

For the next hour or so, David asks me lots of questions, some quite intimate, and some that don't appear to be necessary. He has been on the laptop all this time and we have come up with a few interesting points.

Ethan had carried on dancing after he left me, but his dancing wasn't up to par. He couldn't keep a dance partner as they all kept quitting, citing his bad attitude and his continual obsession with them not being me. I never Googled him after I left the States because I didn't want to see his success without me. Maybe I should have. It would have made me feel a bit better.

He had disappeared off the dance circuit about a year ago, and other than a few articles on him and his disappearance, the trail dies. We don't know where he is or what state of mind he's in.

"I'm going to check on my computer at home. I can look at flight records and security recordings at the airport. We have a rough timescale for when he might have come into the country. It might take me a few hours but I will find him. We have some Google pictures of him. Do you have any that we can see, just so we get a better image of him?"

I nod and climb the stairs. I reach into my bottom drawer and bring out the box of photos that I wanted to throw away so many times, but just couldn't. I wanted something for Gracie to have when she started asking questions about her dad. I pull out my favourite one of us together, when we were happy. We were at the Rockefeller Centre in New York, ice skating one Christmas. It brings back a lot of happy memories, but I push them back. I need to be strong for Gracie.

"Here, have this one," I say, handing it to

David. "I have some for Gracie upstairs." I look at Spence. I don't want him to think I still love Ethan. I don't. I love Spence. He puts his hand on my shoulder as he stands behind me.

"That's perfect. Thank you, Snow. Right, lads. Let's go. Spence, are you coming with us? We might be making a move tonight if we find anything out."

I look up at him and I can see he is torn between wanting to find Gracie and wanting to stay and comfort me. "Go, Spence. You'll find her. I know you'll bring her home to me." He leans down and kisses me, and I feel all his emotions in that one small peck on my lips. Spence loves me and he will do anything to get Gracie back.

"I love you, Snow. I love Gracie too, and I won't let anyone hurt her."

The four of them pack up their laptop and put away their shot glasses before leaving. They say goodbye to my mum as they walk out of the door.

Standing at the door, I watch them leave until their cars have driven down the road so far that I can't see them anymore then I close the door and walk into the lounge. I plonk myself down on the couch with a big sigh.

"Well, that was interesting," Dad says,

holding Mum's hand. "They looked really scary when they walked in, but I don't think I've met a nicer bunch of men!"

"I know. They look mean, and they can be when necessary, but they have our interests at heart. They might be unorthodox, but I don't care as long as Gracie comes back to us."

We sit in the lounge for a couple of hours, talking about Gracie and all the funny things about her. We cry because we miss her and know she will be missing us too. I can't think of her alone, cold and crying for me. It breaks my heart.

We talk about Ethan and why he would do this and not come to me and just ask to see her. In a way, I hope she is with him and it's not just a random kidnapping, because even though he might have done this, I know he wouldn't hurt her. He wouldn't hurt his own flesh and blood. Would he?

Just as we're going to bed, the phone rings. I rush over to it and Mum and Dad stand behind me, waiting to hear some news.

"Snow, this is Detective Fisher. We have no news as yet, and we have already got search parties in the area. As it's getting dark, we have to suspend them until dawn. Have you had any further

developments on your end?"

I try to hold back my tears. I thought they might have something for me. Thank God Sawyer and the guys have taken this on. I'm sure they will move it ahead faster than the police.

"No, nothing. I rang all her friends and no one has seen her since she left ballet class today."

"Listen, we will be in touch the minute we hear something. Try to sleep. You'll need all your strength to get through the next few days."

I hang up. I don't hold out much hope for them being successful. It seems Ethan has covered his tracks very well if the police are not even suspicious of him.

I shake my head at my parents. "No news. It's dark and they can't do any more physical searching. They're going to start again tomorrow morning. I hope Spence has more luck!"

"I'm sure he will. They all seemed very determined to get her found as quickly as possible," Mum says, taking me into a hug.

When I pull away, I say, "I'm off to bed. I

need to try and get some sleep."

We all say goodnight and I head up the stairs. I walk into Gracie's bedroom and sit on her bed. All her teddy bears and dolls are sitting on her bed, and that's when I start to cry. I pull her favourite bear, Popcorn, to me and sniff it.

She smells like Gracie. I smile, recalling the day she got this bear. We were in Hamley's in London and we were visiting Santa Claus. She was so excited, but when she walked into his house, she stopped still and started crying. I never thought about how she would feel being so close to him, but she was totally overwhelmed. She clung onto me so tightly, I didn't know where my leg ended and Gracie began.

I wish she had Popcorn with her right now; she wouldn't feel so alone then.

Santa was really good at his job, and he managed to talk her around. He gave her Popcorn and he said to her, "When you are feeling sad or lonely then you need to give this gorgeous bear a big hug. She will make you feel less lonely and she will give you courage to do whatever you want, Gracie."

As I'm thinking back and smiling at Popcorn, my phone rings. It frightens me a bit, but I see it's Spence's number.

"Have you found her yet?" I ask.

"No, babe. Not yet. I just wanted to check if there was any news your end."

"Nothing. The police rang to say they had to call the search party off as it was getting dark and they will resume in the morning. What am I going to do, Spence? I can't lose her."

"I know, Snow. I don't want to lose her either. She means so much to me after only a short period of time. Listen, if you hear anything, let me know. We're going to pull an all-nighter and see what we can find out. I'll ring you in the morning. Remember I love you."

"I love you too, Spence." I have tears in my eyes, and when he hangs up, I let them come to the surface and spill over. I was so lucky the day I met him.

I make my way into my bedroom and climb into bed. I don't expect to sleep because my mind is racing, but soon the darkness and heaviness in my heart takes over and I drift off.

ETHAN

I run my fingers through my hair, tugging at it to relieve the stress. Why did I do it? Why did I steal my daughter from under Snow's nose? I'm not a horrible person, really I'm not. I just wanted to know her. I wanted a chance to love her. After what I did all those years ago, I didn't think she would let me see her. I did the only thing I could think of. I stole her.

I look over to the single bed in the room and watch Gracie sleeping. I had been watching her for a few weeks, and heard her friends calling her one day. I love that name. It was my grandmother's name. She whimpers in her sleep. "Mummy, help me."

My heart breaks. I shouldn't have taken her. She's only a child, for God's sake. I love her already though, and I want her to know me, to love me back.

I was so surprised when she went to the toilet during class. She doesn't normally do that. Like I said, I've been watching her for a few weeks and she always goes to the toilet at the end of the class. I took the opportunity to speak to her.

"Gracie," I said, as she stopped running and turned to look at me.

"Who are you?" she says, standing there with her hands on her hips.

I chuckled. "I'm a friend of Spencer's. He asked me to collect you."

I had found out Snow's boyfriend's name the other day when I had followed them to the park. Gracie was shouting out his name all the time, so I couldn't really miss it. It had really upset me to see her playing with this guy and smiling at him. It should have been me she was smiling at, not him.

"Mummy didn't say that someone else would collect me. I'll check with Rachel." She turned to go back into class, but I couldn't let that happen, so I just grabbed her, put my hand over her mouth, and held her to me tightly. She struggled against my hold, and when I got her into the car, I put some chloroform, which was already on a cloth, over her mouth and nose. I needed her to not struggle.

It wasn't a long drive, and I carried her inside, hoping that she would stay asleep until I had got her in the basement where no one could hear her screams. I needed her to trust me before I took her upstairs.

I sat on the bed and gently laid her down. She instinctively curled up into a little ball.

It had given me the opportunity to look at her properly. Her coloring is slightly lighter than Snow's. Gracie is more like a very light milk chocolate color. Her hair is not as tight as I thought it would be; it doesn't feel as wiry either. It feels silky soft. She has my eyes. That's the first thing I noticed about her. She has bright blue eyes and they stand out. They are so beautiful.

I don't know what my next move is. I didn't think this through as much as I should have. I know Snow would have relented and let me see her, but I can't see Snow with someone else. It killed me when I saw them together in the park the other day. I still love her and I regret leaving her every day of my life. It has eaten me up inside, and I can't even dance now. It's not the same without her. I can tell she loves Spence. She lights up when she sees him. It breaks my heart to see what I gave up so easily.

I watch Gracie trying to sleep the chloroform off and my heart breaks. Have I just made the second worst mistake of my life?

REALITY KICKS IN

SNOW

I wake up with a start. I look at the clock and see it's only five o'clock. It's still dark outside. While my eyes get used to the dark, I remember Gracie. I jump out of bed and run out of my room and into hers.

"Gracie! Gracie!" I shout as I approach her bed. I reach out and realise she isn't there. She didn't sneak back in during the night when I was asleep. I lay on her bed with Popcorn and sob.

"Snow." I feel a hand on my shoulder, shaking me. "Wake up. Spence is on the phone," Mum says. As I open my eyes and sit up, I see that her eyes look how mine feel. Swollen and red.

"Spence?" I shout into the phone.

"Hey, babe. I just wanted to check up on you. Any news?"

"No, and I'm assuming you don't have any either."

"I'm sorry, no news. Although, Stig jumped up about half an hour ago and ran out of Sawyer's saying, 'I've seen him recently.' We haven't heard from him yet, but I have a feeling this might be a good lead."

"Oh, I hope so, Spence," I say, sobbing. "Let me know when you hear anything, please."

"Of course. I love you."

I hang up, and Mum is looking at me expectantly.

I shake my head. "Nothing yet. Stig thinks he might have seen Ethan recently, but they don't know where he went. He just rushed out of the apartment."

"That could be the lead they need, Snow. Don't give up. They have yours and Gracie's interests at heart."

"I know, Mum. I just don't want to get too excited and get my hopes up for them to fail."

"I know."

I follow her downstairs and see that it's eight o'clock. I must have fallen back asleep.

"What do we do now? I don't think I can hang around waiting. I need to do something."

"There's nothing we can do, Snow. We rang round her friends yesterday. We need to wait for the police."

I stand up and slam my cup down. "I can't just sit here while he just ... just ... I don't know what he's doing to her! She is going to be so scared, Mum!"

"I know she is. We're all scared. I don't think I can live if he hurts her."

ETHAN

I haven't slept all night. I've just been watching Gracie. Watching how she sleeps. She kept crying in her sleep. Tears running down her face. I feel horrible, regretful and downright stupid. Today, I'm determined to show her who I really am and how much I love her, because I do love her so much.

She rolls over and faces the outside of the bed. She opens her eyes and then realizes where she is. She jumps back into the far corner of the bed, pulls her knees up in front her, and wraps her arms around them. "Please don't hurt me. I didn't do anything to make you hate me."

My heart breaks. "I don't hate you, Gracie. I love you."

"No, you don't. Mummy told me that if you love someone then you wouldn't hurt them."

"Your mummy is very clever, but I'm not going to hurt you. I promise. I just want to show you something."

She scoots her bottom forward on the bed. "What do you want to show me?"

I smile at her and reach into the cupboard at the side of the bed and pull out a box. Her eyes open wide when she sees the box. She doesn't know what's in it and it scares her.

"Don't be frightened. This is my memory box. You know what one of those is, don't you?"

She nods her head.

I slowly take the lid off and show her it's full of photographs. The first one lying on the top is one of Snow in her *Swan Lake* outfit. I hand it to her.

She gasps. "It's ... It's Mummy!"

"Yes, it is. Doesn't she look beautiful?"

She nods her head and reaches out to take another picture. This one is of Snow and me at an after-hours party. We were so happy. I catch my breath as she looks at the picture and then looks up at me, and then back down at the photo.

"This is you? With Mummy?"

I nod my head. "Yes, it is. I knew your mummy a long time ago."

"Were you her boyfriend?" she says as she looks through all the pictures in the box. I can see her visibly relax as she realizes I'm not the enemy.

"Yes, I was, but we didn't last."

"You both look so happy. Why didn't it work?"

I laugh. How much will I tell her?

Sixteen

CLOSING IN

SPENCE

We've only had a couple of hours' sleep in the last few days. We're exhausted, but we won't stop until we find Gracie. I won't go to Snow until I know she is safe. I can't. I need her to know that I will do anything for her. I don't want to disappoint her. I need to find Gracie.

Tilda brings us coffee and sets it down on the coffee table in her lounge. "Guys, you really need to sleep. You stink, you've only eaten crap, and you need to spend time with the ones you love!"

David grabs her legs as she starts to move

away from the table. "Baby, I am spending time with the one I love." He pulls her down to sit on his lap and then kisses her. I can't look away, but I'm jealous. I want Snow to come and wrap herself around me. I want her to reassure me that she loves me. I want to reassure her that I love her.

David continues to talk to us, even though Tilda is sitting on his lap. He's rubbing her arse subconsciously.

Watching David makes me miss Snow. I don't think I've gone so long without seeing her since we started dating. I'm just about to text her when Stig comes in the front door.

"Right, you guys need to come down to Whiskey Sour. I've put together some footage you need to see."

I stand. "What kind of footage?"

"This IS going to lead us to Ethan. I can feel it, Spence!" He pulls me to him and slaps me on the back.

David has moved Tilda off his lap. "Come on then. We've no time to waste."

While we're in the car on our way to Whiskey Sour, I text Snow.

"Morning, babe. I've got a feeling today is going to be a good day."

She texts back straight away.

"Morning xx I hope so."

She sounds so sad.

"I'm going to come see you tonight, regardless. Can I stay the night? Will your mum let me?"

"Of course she will. She loves you, but not as much as I do."

"I'll kiss those tears away, babe. I'll see you later."

We pull up outside the club and Stig opens the door for us. Whiskey and Jeannie are waiting for us.

"Spence, how's Snow?" Whiskey asks.

"She's doing okay, but each day she loses more of her sparkle."

"We were thinking of going over to see her. Even if we just sit with her and wait for news. Today is going to be a good day though. I can feel it."

"That's what I said to her this morning, and of course she would love you going over. You're family and she needs support right now. I'm busy trying to find Gracie and I hate myself for not being there with her. But I can help her more by being here and looking for Gracie."

"I know she appreciates everything you're doing, Spence. Now, follow the lads to the security room and let's see if we can find this bastard," Whiskey says, with determination in her voice.

When we get into the security room, all the screens are turned on to make it one huge screen. I take a seat so I'm front and centre.

Stig presses play on the recording that he's compiled. "Okay, it took me a little time before I realised I had seen Ethan before. When Snow showed us the pictures of him, he looked different to how he looks now."

"You've seen him? Where the fuck have you seen him, Stig?" I shout at him.

"Relax, Spence, and watch!"

Sitting back in my chair, I watch the scenes unfold in front of me. There are pictures of Ethan here in Whiskey Sour, watching the girls dancing. He has long hair, a beard, and he looks dirty.

"How did we let him in looking like that?" Whiskey asks. "We have a very strict dress code." She looks at Stig as he is in charge of admissions and subscriptions.

"I don't know. It might have been a really busy night and he came in as a guest with someone else. I can't work out who brought him in yet. But you'd better believe I'm on it."

We continue looking at the screens. It shows

Ethan ordering from me at the bar. He goes back to his seat and watches Snow dancing. He looks like he's in pain. After the show you can see him watching her wherever she goes. He watches her as she comes up to the bar and kisses me; it's a ritual that she does. He leaves at that point of the evening. He'd seen enough.

I'm about to say something to Stig when the screen moves onto another night. Oh my God; he came here a few times. He looks cleaner this time. We see him signing in at the reception area and talking to Stig.

"Fuck, Stig!" Sawyer says.

"I know."

We watch as he repeats exactly what he did the previous time he was in. He talks to me at the bar and then watches Snow.

"Oh my God. I think I remember him now." I shake my head. "He was talking to me, telling me he was on holiday from the States and that the girls were amazing. I told him that Snow was my girlfriend and he heard her calling me Spence. That's how he must have known my name when he went to collect Gracie." I shake my head. How could I not have remembered him?

"So, we vaguely remember seeing him," Sawyer says, while Stig has paused the recording. "How does this help us catch him though, Stig?"

"He had to give us an address when he came in as a guest, and also when he signed up for membership. I went through the footage bit by bit until I could match the members with their visitors and then I found his. From the night he first came here and then when he signed up as a member." At this point, Stig is holding a file in the air. He is meticulous with the members because sometimes a weirdo can turn up and we need to avoid any scenes or trouble.

I reach up to grab it, but he just lifts it higher. "Obviously, I have gone through his file and application, and yes, I do have an address. He had given a hotel address when he came in as someone's guest, but when he applied for membership he put a different address. I've watched him on the security cameras outside the club and he seems to walk in the same direction every time. The address he gave is in that direction, so I can only assume he put the right address down."

David stands up. "So, what are we waiting for?"

Sawyer stands up as well and says, "We need to decide how we do this, David. We know your methods, and although they have worked in the past, there is a child involved here. We need to decide if we go to the police, or do we go in ourselves? Whatever we do, we need to avoid any violence in front of Gracie. Understood?"

We all nod and say yes. "Can I see the address please, Stig?"

He hands me the file and I open it carefully. I recognise the address, or at least the area. "This isn't that far from here. I can't sit here and not rush over to Gracie. Please tell me we won't be sitting here for the rest of the day."

Sawyer chuckles. "No, Spence. We won't be sitting here all day, but we need to do this right. We need to work out a plan and we have to remember that Gracie's safety is our only concern. Spence, you need to come with us so she knows someone and feels comfortable coming with us."

"Of course I'm going to be there. There is nothing that would stop me from getting Gracie out of his clutches and taking her home to Snow."

"Right then. Let's do this right. We only get one chance before the police have to be involved."

Seventeen

FAMILY

SNOW

The bell rings and I run to open the door. Whiskey is standing there with Jeannie and Tilda. She pulls me into a hug, and I'm so happy to see them all.

"Come in. Thanks for coming to see me."

"You're one of us. You're family, Snow. Get the kettle on. We want to tell you what we've just seen."

I open my mouth to say something when she pushes me inside and towards the kitchen.

"Kettle!" She laughs.

I turn it on and then look at them

expectantly. "What did you see, Whiskey? You can't hold out on me now." I busy myself with getting cups and making coffee. My heart is pounding. My hands are shaking. I need to know what's going on.

"Well, you know Spence has been with the guys at Tilda's place? They've been following up leads, which basically have been dead ends. Stig went over this morning and he brought them all back to the club. He has spent the last day or so piecing together all the parts of this very intricate puzzle."

I sit down at the table after giving them all their coffee. I feel sick. Are we going to find her today? I just want to know she is safe and that we are going to find her.

"And?"

"They think they have an address. Ethan had been to the club a few times, and he applied for a membership," Jeannie says. She would know; she works in the membership office with Stig when she's not dancing.

"He's been in the club. What the fuck?" I can't believe he was there and I didn't know.

"Yeah, a few times. Anyway, we found his application form and the guys are on their way over to the address to see if they can find Gracie. They are going to be careful so that they don't frighten her, but this could be it, Snow. Gracie could be coming home today."

I flop in my chair, lay my head on the table, and sob. My baby might be coming home today!

Mum and Dad have come into the kitchen, and the girls are telling them what they know. Dad puts his hand on my shoulder from behind me, and Mum sits down at the table next to me; she is crying too.

SPENCER

My heart is beating so fast it feels like it's going to jump out of my chest. I used to feel like this all the time before, when I was living on adrenaline and fear. We're in David's car, on our way to find Gracie, or at least to where we think she is. If she's not there then we will have to go to the police with our evidence and let them find her. This is our last ditch attempt to find her

"Spence, are you listening?" David asks me irritably.

"Sorry, David. I'm nervous and excited. I haven't done anything like this for a few years.

"I know, Spencer, and we're sorry to drag

you into this but you're the best one to be there for Gracie so she doesn't get scared."

"I know. I'll be fine. I just need to find her. Snow isn't far off a nervous breakdown and it's horrible to watch. She's usually such a strong woman."

Everyone nods and agrees.

It's quiet for about a minute then David says, "Right, we need to go over the plan so we all know what's going to happen. Spence, you have to take the lead on this one, I'm afraid. Knock on the door, and when he opens it, just push past him and call out for Gracie. Find her and make sure she's not hurt."

"Right. It'll be hard not to fucking kill him though, but I understand."

David chuckles. "Stig, I want you in next, straight behind Spence. You need to restrain Ethan. Make sure he doesn't bolt out the door. With your build and stature, he won't be able to get past you. Just in case he does, I'll be right behind you. Sawyer, you're the talker. You need to question him and find out what the hell he's been doing and what he thinks his next move is. We DON'T hurt him, right?"

We all grumble. I know I won't be able to keep my hands off him, but I don't need to tell

David that. He knows it, but chooses to ignore it.

"Sawyer, find out what you can then we will get Gracie back to Snow. She is going to have to meet with Ethan though."

"Why the fuck does she have to see that toerag after everything he has done to her and Gracie?" I can feel my blood boiling.

"Spence. Gracie is his daughter," Sawyer says.

"Yeah, but he never wanted her, so he can fuck off out of her life."

"Look, you're emotional because of how you feel about Gracie and Snow."

Sawyer is pissing me off now.

"Are you seriously telling me that if Whiskey had a child and someone took her, that you would just shake his hand and say 'see you around' because I don't think so!"

"Okay, you've got a point. At the end of the day, Snow will have to decide if she presses charges or not."

"Right, guys. We're here. Are you ready? It's the house with the blue door, number 224. Spence, are you ready?"

I'm out of the car already and storming towards the door.

"Spence, slow down! Wait for us to be your

back up."

I slow down but don't say anything. I stand in front of the blue door and wait, patiently, for the rest to catch up. I'm tapping my foot, trying to get rid of some of my anxiety.

Stig comes up behind me and taps me on the shoulder. "Right, Spence. This is it. Let's go!"

I take a deep breath and make the sign of the cross as I always did before going into battle. I knock really hard on the door and then I wait. My heart is making as much noise as my knock on the door did. I wait … and wait …Then I knock again.

This time I hear a door being unbolted. Someone's mumbling, "Alright, I'm coming!"

The door is opened a fraction, and two eyes appear in front of me. "What do you want?"

"Ethan? Ethan Cross? Is that you?" I ask, trying to keep my temper at bay.

"Who are you? I don't know you." I see the moment when he recognises me and the guys stood behind me. He tries to close the door in my face.

I push the door open so that I can see the owner of the two eyes. Yep, it's Ethan. "You little fucker. You messed with the wrong people this time, Ethan." I can see the shock in his eyes as he gets pushed back against the wall. He recognised us from the club, and now he's scared.

"Where's Gracie? If you've hurt her or touched ..." I spit at him in disgust. "So help me God!"

"She's ... She's downstairs. I haven't touched her, I promise. I just wanted to get to know her." He's shaking. I have my hand on his chest and start to walk past him. At the last minute, I lean forward and head butt him. I can't help myself. He starts crying and holds his head.

"SPENCE, there's no time! Go find Gracie!" Stig pushes me into the house.

"Gracie!" I'm standing in the middle of what looks like a lounge. "Gracie!" I look around for a door which will take me downstairs. I finally see it in the kitchen, and I open it and scream down the stairs, "GRACIE!"

I hear something from down below. "Spence? Is that you?"

"Yeah, Gracie, it's me. I'm coming down."

I run down the stairs and she's running towards the bottom of the stairs. She throws herself at me and starts crying. I hold her really tight; I don't want to let her go. I rub her head while she cries on my shoulder. I walk over to the little bed that is in the corner of the room and I sit down. She is still hugging me, but she's stopped crying. It's in this moment that I realise how much I love her. My heart is racing and I just want to protect her.

I pull her away from my shoulder and look at her. She doesn't look hurt. There are no cuts or bruises, anyway. "Gracie, are you hurt?"

She shakes her head. "No. Can I see Mummy now?"

She throws herself at me again, hugging me.

"I'm going to take you to Mummy as soon as I can. Just tell me that he didn't hurt you."

"No, Spencer. I promise he didn't hurt me. He was very nice. We talked a lot about Mummy."

"Thank God he didn't hurt you, Gracie. I don't know what I would have done if he did."

I look around the room and see boxes lying around. The lid is off one of them and it's full of photographs. Then I see some on the bed. "What are these photographs?"

She smiles and bounces off my lap, leans over, and picks up one of Snow and Ethan on the stage together. They look so happy. They look in love. I start to have strange feelings. I'm jealous of them. I'm jealous of Ethan. I've never been jealous before in my whole life. I don't like the feeling.

"It's Mummy and Ethan; look at them dancing together." She is smiling and pointing at the picture while looking at me.

I force a smile. "Oh, yeah. Look at them. They look great."

"He knew Mummy a long time ago and he just wanted to see her again." She lowers her voice. "Spencer, can I tell you a secret?"

I lower mine too. "Of course you can, Gracie. You can tell me anything."

She looks around the room and then she kneels on the bed and cups her hand around her mouth and leans into my ear. Very gently and quietly, she says, "Ethan told me that he is my dad, but that it is a secret and I'm not to tell anyone. I wanted to tell you though."

"He told you that?" I ask incredulously.

"Yeah, that's why he wanted to meet me. I told him he could have just come to the house." She puts the photograph back in the box.

"Yeah, he could have. That would have been easier. So, he definitely didn't hurt you?"

"No, Spencer. I promise."

I smile at her. "Okay, then. Let's go and find Mummy and she can decide what happens next. Okay?"

She starts to jump up and down on the bed. "Yay, let's go." When she jumps off the bed, she reaches down and takes the box of photographs.

"What are you doing with them?" I ask.

"I'm taking them so that when Ethan comes over, he can go through them with Mummy." In her mind, it makes perfect sense. He is now her dad and she is going to see him all the time. I just hope she doesn't think that he's going to get back with Snow and they can all live happily ever after. I don't want that to happen. Then again, who am I to stop them being a happy family?

I shake my head to get rid of those horrible thoughts. "Come on then. Let's go."

I carry her upstairs, and as we walk through the lounge, I see Ethan sitting in a chair, surrounded by all three of the guys. Poor man; he looks petrified.

"Spence, is she okay?" Sawyer asks.

"Yeah, she's fine. I'm taking the car. I need to get her home to Snow. I'll ring you when I've spoken to her, so you know what to do with HIM!"

"Okay, let us know. Good luck!"

"Thanks. I'm going to need it," I say, as I walk towards the door.

Gracie shouts out, "Bye, Ethan! Sorry ... Daddy. See you later."

REUNITED

SNOW

Spencer just rang and told me he is on his way back to the house with Gracie. I spoke to her and she sounds fine. I'm pacing the floors just waiting for them to come back. I missed her so much. I can't wait to smother her with kisses.

Mum and Dad are looking out the front window with me when we see a car pull up. The driver door opens, and Spence gets out and walks round to the passenger side. When he opens the door, he lets Gracie climb up onto his back and he brings her to the house. I have the door open before he even gets here and I have tears streaming down my face.

"Mummy! Mummy!" Spence has to let her down because she wants to run to me.

She runs so fast she almost knocks me over. "Baby, oh my God! Baby girl." I hug her so tight I think I might suffocate her.

I can't believe she's home. It's been four days and I missed her so much. I reach out and grab Spence to bring him into our hug. "I love you even more, Spence. Thank you for bringing her home to me. I won't ever forget it." I kiss him on the cheek.

"I love you both," he says, hugging us tight.

When we pull away, Mum and Dad come up behind us and Gracie runs to them and throws herself at them. There are a lot of tears.

"He didn't hurt her, Snow. He said he just wanted to meet her. He looked awful," I whisper. "She knows he's her daddy." I stand upright and look into her eyes. I see a flash of worry in them. She is obviously worried about what is going to happen now, and what he might have said to her.

"Oh no! She never asked about her daddy so I hadn't told her anything. Was she upset?"

"No, she seemed to like him. He had a box full of photographs of you and him and she was showing them to me." I try not to show

Snow that I was jealous; it really isn't the time. "She brought the box home with her."

"Oh God. Maybe I should have contacted him. He's her daddy, after all. He has rights."

"Listen, Snow," I say, putting my hands on her shoulders so she stops worrying and looks at me. "He walked out on you at a time when you needed him the most. It's his own fault he hasn't got to know her before now, not yours."

She hangs her head and leans into me. "I know that, Spence, but I could have avoided all of this."

"NO! *He* could have avoided all of this if he had stepped up once you had her. Don't take the blame for this. You've done nothing wrong."

She wraps her hands around my neck and I pull her tight. I don't want to let her go. I have a feeling things are going to change and I'm not sure it's going to be for the best.

"We need to talk about Ethan, babe. What do you want to do now? The guys are with him back at his place. They have him restrained, but they aren't going to take him to the police until you've decided what to do."

"I forgot about them! What do I need to do, Spence? I suppose I need to see him."

"Yeah, you do, but you don't have to do it

alone. I can be there, the guys can be there, your parents can be there. You need to decide what you want to do about the police. They've been looking for Gracie for the last four days and we need to let them know she is home and safe."

"Fuck, Spence. I didn't think of that. What am I going to do?" She puts her head into her hands.

"I'll ring the police if you want, and tell them that she's home safe and sound and you'll speak to them tomorrow after she's settled back in the house. As long as they know she's safe, they should be okay about that." He kisses me on the forehead and walks away from me to make the call.

I don't know how I would have got through this week without Spence, I really don't. I turn to look at Mum and Dad and Gracie. I smile and walk over to them, and ask Gracie, "Are you okay, baby? Are you tired? Are you hurt?"

"No, Mummy." She laughs. "Ethan wouldn't hurt me. We had fun. He was telling me lots of stories about you and your dancing."

"Did he? I bet that was lots of fun."

"Yeah, it was. When can I see him again, Mummy? He told me he is my daddy," she says, with a huge smile on her face.

"We'll talk about it, baby girl, I promise. Tonight, we need to just spend time with you and make sure you're okay. We missed you so much, Gracie." I hug her. I find it hard to leave her alone. I just want to touch her.

Spence walks back into the room. "I've talked to the police and they're going to come out first thing in the morning."

"Thanks, Spence," Dad says, shaking his hand.

He looks at me and says, "Right, I'm going to leave you all to make sure Gracie is okay, and I'll be back in the morning before the police come back, I promise."

"No," all of us say at the same time.

"Spence, you have to stay with us tonight. You brought Gracie home to us. You're family," Mum says to him before I get chance to say anything.

He looks at me and I nod, with tears running down my face. My Mum loves him too. We all love him.

"Then I'd love to stay. Gracie, how about you show us the pictures in the box and the stories that go with them," he says, picking up the box from the table and handing it to Gracie. She smiles at him when she takes it and then she walks ahead of all of us into the lounge.

I stand at the door and watch them take a seat around the table. Mum and Dad are watching Gracie with smiles on their faces. Spence is hooked on each word she says. This is family; this is home.

Gracie looks up at me, smiles, and holds her hand out to me. "Come on, Mummy. Look at this picture! You look so funny."

I laugh and walk towards the people I love most in the world.

Nineteen

FIVE YEARS LATER

SNOW

"Mummy, Mummy! Do I look pretty?" Gracie asks, as she spins around and her dress stands out.

"Gracie, you look so gorgeous. I love your dress," I tell her.

"Daddy bought it for me. He said you would love it and it matches the colour of your dress too."

I laugh. "Daddy always did have good taste. Are you excited for today?"

"I can't wait, Mummy. Daddy's going to meet us at the church and I know what I have to do. I have to sprinkle the rose petals as I walk to the front. Then I can sit down on the front row. That's right, isn't it?"

"Yeah, baby, that's right. Are you not nervous?"

"No. I can't wait to do our dance that we practised. I think he will love it, Mummy."

"I think so too. Now let me finish getting ready. It wouldn't be good to be late."

An hour later, we're standing at the back of the church. I peek through the door and see Ethan standing there in his suit; he looks so handsome. I smile and gently close the door. "Now, baby, the music is going to start in a minute and then I'll open the door for you. I'll follow you down in a few minutes, okay? I'll be behind you, baby. You'll be great.

"Okay, let's do this," I say, as I hear the first few bars of *The Wedding March* being played. I kiss Gracie and hold the door open for her so she can walk in front of me down the aisle. She looks gorgeous and so grown up. I have a tear in my eye. God, I'm so emotional, but then again, I am pregnant, so I'm allowed to be hormonal.

Closing the door behind me, I take a deep breath and lean against it. When I open my eyes, Camille is there in front of me, smiling.

"Are you okay, Snow?"

"Yeah, Camille. I'm just so happy for Ethan. He deserves some happiness in his life, and you are the perfect match for him. You make Gracie so happy and treat her so well. Thank you."

"She's a lovely kid, Snow. Thank you for letting Ethan see her after what he did. Not a day goes by when he doesn't regret what he did."

"I know, but at least it brought them back together. Now, let me creep in and get my seat next to Spence and I'll see you later when you're Mrs Cross." I lean forward to kiss this amazingly beautiful woman who is Gracie's stepmother.

Opening the door again, I sneak down to where Spence is sitting. He smiles when he looks up at me, and when I sit down, he puts his arm around my shoulders and pulls me closer. "Gracie looks so gorgeous. I can't wait to see you two dance together."

"Thanks, babe. I'm so excited too."

He places his free hand on my stomach. "Are you sure it's okay to dance? Will Junior be okay?"

I laugh. "Junior? Really?"

"Well, until we know the sex of this one, I

think Junior is appropriate." He laughs and rubs my stomach.

Camille looks gorgeous as she walks down the aisle, and everything about the wedding is beautiful. Not as beautiful as my wedding to Spence. That was an amazing day.

All the Whiskey Sour crew were there, and no one can say it was a boring day. There was obviously lots of dancing and lots of drinking. There was a lot of sex as well, because a month after the wedding, I found out I was pregnant with Millie. At first we thought Gracie was going to be pissed off, but she took to the role of big sister so well.

After Spence brought Gracie home to us, we told the police that she had run away with her dad. We told them that he brought her home after a couple of days. He was questioned but I didn't press charges because at the end of the day he is her dad. We didn't want Ethan to get into trouble. I think he had enough trouble when he was being 'detained' by Sawyer and the guys. He apologised profusely, and we had a few meetings without Gracie. He told me that he had felt so guilty about leaving me back in New York, but he hadn't thought I would let him see her and he got desperate.

He promised us that he would go to

therapy, and we started off with supervised visits, and then eventually she was able to stay overnight. We knew he wasn't going to do anything stupid, but it took me a long time to be able to let her go without worrying whether she was going to come back or not. I know I was stupid, but he needed to prove himself.

Spence, on the other hand, was a different story. He stayed that night with us, but he let Gracie sleep with me. When I woke up the next morning, he was gone. I didn't know what to think, and he avoided my calls and took time off work.

I went into Whiskey Sour a week later and stormed into the security office.

"Sawyer, where the fuck is he and why isn't he talking to me? What the fuck did I do?"

I didn't see Whiskey was in the room, but she stood up and said, "I told you he was wrong, Sawyer. Sort it the fuck out!" She turned to me, stuck her index finger in my face, and said, "Don't ever barge into my office again!" Then she walked out.

"Sawyer, please. I'm begging you. You guys helped to bring my Gracie home. I love you all. But I need Spence. He's my rock and he keeps me sane. I can't do this without him." I break down and fall to

the floor.

"Fuck!" he says, as he pulls me up off the floor and hugs me. "You women drive me fucking crazy. Let me ring him to come and get you. He needs to sort this shit out, not me!" I sob, but I hear him on the phone. "Spence, get your ass down here and take your girl home. She needs you. Why the fuck are you not here already?" He hangs up.

"Snow, listen to me. Spence went through some shit when we first met him, and going into Ethan's place affected him a lot. He hurt Ethan, but he wanted to hurt him a lot more. He restrained himself and now he's had to step away for the week to control his temper. He's on his way. He can talk to you himself."

"I don't care what he's done in the past, I care about what he wants to do in the future. I owe him so much."

"I know, babe." He picks up the phone and rings down to the bar. "Bring us two drinks, please. A Whiskey Sour for me and a Sex on a Snowbank for Snow."

The drinks arrive a few minutes later, and as I'm downing mine, Spence runs in. I just sit there looking at him.

"Babe, I'm sorry." He kneels down in front of me and takes my hands in his. He kisses them. "Don't cry, please."

Sawyer stands up. "I'm going to find my wife and take her down to the basement and fuck her bad mood out of her." He walks out and closes the door.

"Spence, why did you leave me? I needed you and you weren't there. I never thought you wouldn't be there for me."

"Babe, I had to leave to sort my head out. My life wasn't good before Stig found me and brought me here, and all that aggression with Ethan and thinking about what he had done to Gracie nearly pushed me over the edge. I didn't want to fall apart around you when you needed to be strong."

"But, Spence, I'm not strong without you by my side."

He shakes his head, stands up, and starts pacing around the office. "Fuck! I didn't want to watch you play happy families with Ethan, alright!" He's shouting and pulling at his hair. "I didn't want to see you go back to him! I heard Gracie talking about him and I could hear how much she loves him already. That broke my heart that she loved the man who took her away from her family when I love her so much. I couldn't stop you from giving her her happy ending, Snow. She deserves it so much. So much more than I do!"

I think my heart just broke. I stand up and walk over to him. This time, I take his hands in mine and I kiss them. I push him up against the wall. His eyes open wide and he looks at me. I point my index finger at him and shout, "I ... Love ... You." I prod him with each word. "Gracie ... loves ... you." I punch him with each word. "We needed you this week. I needed you. Gracie hasn't stopped asking for you. You are her hero. You are my hero. How can you even think I would want Ethan over you?"

"He's Gracie's father, Snow. That can't be undone."

"I know that, Spence, but you're the person she loves and misses so much, not him. She doesn't know him. Please come home with me." I look up into his eyes and he has tears in them. I stand on my tiptoes, lean forward, and kiss him gently.

He growls and then grabs my body and slams it into his and devours my mouth. I moan. I've missed his lips. I've missed his body. I've missed him.

"I love you, Snow, I didn't want to lose you to him, but I wanted to give you the space you might need to sort things out with him. If you wanted to be with Ethan to make Gracie happy, then I was preparing myself to walk away."

"But it's you I want, Spence. I told you that before."

He turns me around so my back is against the wall. "I need you, Snow. I need to be inside you right now!"

"What are you waiting for?" I ask, smiling into

his mouth. I reach down and undo his belt on his jeans and then undo the buttons. I put my hand inside his boxers and feel how hard he is for me. I wrap my hand around his enlarged cock and hear him groan. I pull his boxers down low enough that it springs to life. He lifts me up and wraps my legs around his waist. Then he pushes my pants to one side and thrusts inside me.

"Oh my God, Spence. That feels so good."

"It feels like home. I love you." He fucks me hard against the wall and I know it's more than just a fuck, it's him possessing me. He's making sure I know that I am his and no one else's. I don't want to be anyone else's. I just want to be his.

SPENCE

Gracie is the most beautiful flower girl I have ever seen, and I thank my lucky stars that I have her in my life. There was a time when I didn't think she would be a part of my life anymore and it nearly broke me.

I feel a warm hand on my leg and I look up to see Snow smiling at me. We've had the meal and the speeches, and they are about to do the first dance. Camille and Ethan dance their first dance together as man and wife. It's beautiful, and halfway through the song, Snow grabs my hand and drags me on the floor to dance with them.

When the song is over, Snow and Gracie speak to the DJ and they stand in the middle of the now cleared dance floor. The music starts and they both dance to *The Nutcracker*. They are fluid dancing together, and so beautiful. I will never tire of watching Snow dance, whether it is her amazing ballet or her routines at Whiskey Sour; I'm mesmerised every time. They get a standing ovation, and Gracie is so happy. She runs over to me. "Daddy, did you watch that?"

"I did, baby girl. You were gorgeous as always." I whisper in her ear, "You were better than Mummy, but don't tell her I said that."

She kisses me on the cheek and says, "Your secret's safe with me." Then she giggles and runs over to Ethan.

She started calling me Daddy quite soon after the incident with Ethan.

I remember the day well. She came and sat down next to me, and apparently, she had asked everyone else to leave the room for five minutes. We had talked to her about Snow and her moving in with me permanently so that we could be a family, and she was very excited, and this is what I thought she wanted to talk about.

"Spence?"

"Yes, Gracie."

"Can I ask you a question?"

I laugh. "You just did."

"No, another one."

"Of course you can, baby."

"You know now that we are moving in with you? I just ... I just wondered if you would mind if I called you Daddy." She looks up at me with wide eyes that look like they could turn teary any minute.

I'm stunned. I don't know what to say. This little girl has just broken my heart and fixed it in two seconds flat. I can't stop myself getting teary. "Of course you can, Gracie. You don't need to ask." I hug her and she cries. "You know that Ethan is your daddy though, don't you?"

"Yes, of course I do, but I'm special. I have two daddies that love me." And just like that, in the mind of a child, I have become a daddy.

The night is coming to a close, and Gracie is staying with her grandparents tonight. Snow and I are off to Whiskey Sour for our own celebrations. We say goodnight to everyone and grab a cab over to the club.

Everyone welcomes us. We have drinks and dance and sing a little. Before we know it, they're asking Snow to get up on stage and show them the dance that she did with Gracie. She blushes, but she stands on that stage like the professional she is. She has everyone in tears with her beautiful dance, and once again, I am blown away by my wife and mother of my children.

SNOW

Everyone is clapping for the second time tonight, and I feel really emotional. I start to cry, and when I walk over to the bar, everyone starts laughing.

Whiskey says, "Oh God, I forgot you were pregnant. Are we going to have to cope with you crying all the time until you have this child?"

I nod my head; I can't speak.

"Oh, God forgive me, but you need to keep your legs closed, Snow. I don't know if I can cope with your kind of pregnancy crazy again." She laughs.

I look around at these people who are part of my family. I love each and every one of them, and I wouldn't be the person I am today if it wasn't for Whiskey taking a chance on a ballet dancer and seeing the real me inside. Whiskey Sour has become my therapy, my salvation, my everything!

Acknowledgements

There are so many people to acknowledge that I don't like to name people as I might miss someone out.

However, I need to give a shout out and a huge thank you to Jade from SteamPower Studios for taking my visions for the covers of Whiskey Sour and making them so much better than I believed they could be.

Jade seems to understand exactly what I want and I think sometimes I stretch her imagination too.

You've brought these stories alive with your

amazing covers, thank you.

About the Author

I hated English at school! Really hated it! I gave up on English Literature in fourth year because I hated writing stories; couldn't make them up to save my life. I hated writing precis and I was horrendous at grammar. Having lived in Norway when I was younger, English was my second language.

When I received my iPad six years ago I started reading on the kindle app and wrote to an author about how much I enjoyed her book. That opened up the whole facebook author world to me. I started reviewing books (ironic, right?) and then started beta reading (even more ironic) after pointing out some big mistakes in a book plot I was reviewing before release.

I realised I had a story in me, yeah I know everyone says that, but I really believed I did. Eleven books later .... Welcome to the world of Krissy V!